'This lucidly written and deceptively simple narrative by the highly regarded Northern Irish novelist David Park is the story of a troubled journey into the self and out into the world again, towards some glimmer of generosity and redemption' *Sunday Times*

'Sombre, but unsolemn, with a redemptive, tingling finale, this is a small book bursting with big emotions' Anthony Cummins, *Daily Mail*

'There is no false piety in this sometimes desperate, always measured novel, but a compassionately observed, manifestly flawed redemption, akin to what Emily Dickinson referred to as 'the Hour of Lead': a process of mourning that results in a final relinquishing, and an eventual thaw' *Irish Times*

'A father and son novel of rare intensity. We are taken on an unforgettable winter journey and, like in a skid, we have no idea which way we'll be facing by the end. He writes with a focus and precision which wrings the heart' Bernard MacLaverty

'A journey filled with ghostly voices and regret . . . A quietly tense circadian novel with Northern Ireland at its heart . . . Park excels at describing the landscape of Belfast' *Times Literary Supplement*

'Its concerns are firmly on one man and his search for meaning and solace. I was reminded of Mike McCormack's much-praised novel *Solar Bones*' *Irish Independent*

'It is time to call David Park what he is – a very great writer. *Travelling in a Strange Land* is an eruption of love and sorrow, overwhelmingly compassionate and wise, hearing the heart break and maybe even heal, bearing the deepest testimony to the love, unending love, binding parent and child. A mighty book' Frank McGuinness

'I just loved the David Park. Everything about it. It's just a profound and beautifully sad work and if you want to know what great writing is, it's right there' Niall MacMonagle

'David Park's *Travelling in a Strange Land* features a family in crisis in a frozen landscape' *Irish Times*, Books to look out for in 2018

'David Park has written a troubled tale about haunted families which will leave a mark on modern Irish literature ... That this father and son odyssey should come to rest under an angel's wings is just one of its great emotional and artistic rewards. This is possibly Park's best yet, and shines like a beacon' *Big Issue in Scotland*

'Regardless of personal recognition, really good writing forces the best from its readers – namely an honest, if not always comforting, response. *Travelling in a Strange Land* demands soul-searching. A lyrical meditation on instinct, estrangement and connection, it recognises the complexities inherent in all enduring relationships, pre-eminently those between parent and child' *Country Life*

'One of the strongest and truest observers of life, and especially the peculiarities of life in Northern Ireland ... He is compelling on his favourite subject, the delicate balance which ties, and taunts, fathers and sons. This touching story of a ruminating father's solitary journey to Scotland to bring home his sick son for Christmas is one of his best yet. It has all of Park's magic, melancholy and tenderness, and is, in more ways than one, an absolute dream' Jane Graham, *Big Issue*

'I'm always amazed by writers whose work is tightly but perfectly written, as in, they've used the most appropriate wording and can create a world with sparse language.... Mesmerising' *Woman's Way*

DAVID PARK has written ten previous books including *The Big Snow*, *Swallowing the Sun*, *The Truth Commissioner*, *The Light of Amsterdam*, which was shortlisted for the 2014 International IMPAC Prize, and *The Poets' Wives*, which was selected as Belfast's Choice for One City One Book 2014. He has won the Authors' Club First Novel Award, the Bass Ireland Arts Award for Literature, the Ewart-Biggs Memorial Prize, the American Ireland Fund Literary Award and the University of Ulster's McCrea Literary Award, three times. He has received a Major Individual Artist Award from the Arts Council of Northern Ireland and been shortlisted for the Irish Novel of the Year Award three times. In 2014 he was longlisted for the *Sunday Times* EFG Short Story Award. He lives in County Down, Northern Ireland.

Travelling in a Strange Land

David Park

BLOOMSBURY PUBLISHING
LONDON · OXFORD · NEW YORK · NEW DELHI · SYDNEY

BLOOMSBURY PUBLISHING
Bloomsbury Publishing Plc
50 Bedford Square, London, WC1B 3DP, UK
29 Earlsfort Terrace, Dublin 2, Ireland

BLOOMSBURY, BLOOMSBURY PUBLISHING and the Diana logo are
trademarks of Bloomsbury Publishing Plc

First published in Great Britain 2018
This edition published 2018

A catalogue record for this book is available from the British Library.

ISBN: HB: 978-1-4088-9278-7; EBOOK: 978-1-4088-9276-3;
PB: 978-1-4088-9275-6

6 8 10 9 7

Typeset by Newgen Knowledge Works Pvt Ltd., Chennai, India
Printed and bound in Great Britain by CPI Group (UK) Ltd, Croydon CR0 4YY

To find out more about our authors and books visit
www.bloomsbury.com and sign up for our newsletters

To James and Sophie
with a father's love

The photographer must have and keep in him something of the receptiveness of the child who looks at the world for the first time or of the traveller who enters a strange country.

Bill Brandt

I am entering the frozen land, although to which country it belongs I cannot say. Sometimes I see it as from a drone, so down below unravels a snow-smothered terrain of mountains, ravines and lakes, forests that suddenly rear up and brush their whitened branches against my eyes. At other times I am sunk knee-deep in its depths with no horizon visible, struggling to continue on a journey whose purpose is unclear and I do not know where I've come from or where I'm going. The world is covered, its life slowly suffocated like the sheep trapped in deep drifts against ancient stone walls and which I cannot pull free. Everything is hidden, even the secrets that I hug tightly to stop them finding the light, and the world stretches so infinite that I can't reduce it to a single frame and when I narrow my eyes it is only to shut out the wind-driven snow. All things must have a purpose and I must find mine or yield to this frozen land's urging that I should surrender to my weariness and rest my head on the soft pillow of its snow. Bruegel's trudging hunters who return from foraging for food in the wilderness beyond the village are also weary, but the people sporting on the frozen lake don't rush to greet them or understand anything of what they have endured. The Revenant returns to take revenge on the man who killed his son.

Everything must have a purpose. So what is it brings me on this journey?

I stumble snow-blind, fearful that at any moment I might fall into some gaping crevice or step off the cliff face into a sudden shock of space, hands flailing as they try to clutch something on which to hold. Something to stop the endless drop. And then I've reached the edge of the lake and my eyes are clear again so I see the scree of ice trembling under the sheen of moonlight with its scatter of frozen crystals mirroring the stars. Stars whose coldness seems to burn holes in the arching darkness.

There on the far shore stands a house. A house with a light burning. In the house are stairs that I know I shall have to climb. But how do I reach it except across this frozen lake? And who will take my hand? Who will guide me now? I look behind me but hear only the wind as it seethes through the trees, smoking spindrift and making the whole world shiver.

Together we scoop the thick wedge of snow from the car's windscreen. On the surface it's still soft, suggesting that more has fallen during the early hours of the morning, but when our gloved hands finally reach the glass they find a frozen smear that I spray with de-icer. Before opening the door to start the engine and blow hot air against the windscreen I scrape as much snow as I can from the side and back windows, while Lorna uses the long-handled brush to clear the bonnet and roof until grey metal slowly appears. Our breath forms opaque speech bubbles on our lips even though no words pass between us as the early-morning light begins to work itself inside the surface of the snow so that it seems to pulse. But no trace of any form of life is warmed into being and the silent fields surrounding the house are marked only by the skittering night tracks of some creature in a confused pursuit of food.

When I open the car door, the lock grinds in a semi-frozen complaint and a little spray of snow falls on the driver's seat and I try to brush it away with my hand but only succeed in turning it into dark spots of water. Lorna gets in the passenger seat and we sit in the iced car as if in an igloo, blind to the world, and for just a second it feels safe, as if we are protected from everything that lies outside.

'This is crazy, Tom,' she almost shouts over the blast of the heater.

'What choice do we have?'

'Perhaps the planes will start flying soon. I think this is too dangerous,' she says as she tilts the blower vent against her window.

'We can't leave him there. We have to bring him home.'

We sit and stare at the windscreen. A widening strip clears closest to the vents. The sound of the blower roars in my ears.

'You've set the satnav?'

'Yes.'

'And you've got everything?' she asks, glancing over her shoulder at the back seat. 'I'll bring out the flasks and the food in a minute.'

'Yes, I think so,' and I mentally itemise the amateur survival kit we've put together the previous night – the spade, the sleeping bag, the warm clothing, the torch, the pile of CDs, and my camera of course will be there, as it always is. In the boot a plastic canister of petrol and, for some bizarre reason I can't quite fathom, our ten-year-old daughter Lilly's brown canvas wigwam complete with painted horses, moons and stars. She had insisted even when I told her you could spit through it and I had no energy to argue any further. Her snowman still stands sentinel in the front garden like a nightwatchman.

'You'll keep in touch,' Lorna says for about the fourth time. 'And you've got the phone charger?'

I nod as another patch of windscreen clears.

'A watched kettle never boils,' I say, moving my head towards the glass as if my breath might speed the process.

'What time does the boat go?'

'Seven thirty. Should be plenty of time,' and then I add 'all being well' because, with unprecedented falls of snow and the whole country frozen into immobility, nothing seems quite certain any more, and not just the relationship between time and distance but everything that makes up the world as we once thought of it feels like it has been knocked out of sync.

A small hole appears on the glass and if I were on my own I would put my eye to it, stare into the milky light through this little lens. It's how I spend my days, how I look at the world. Round it the ice is loosening and turning slushy. Light seeps in. There have been days recently when I've thought I'm not much more than some little pinhole hoping for the world's image to finally form into permanence rather than this wavering unpredictable flux I feel inside. Growing impatient I turn on the wipers but at first nothing happens before they reluctantly shudder and scud across the screen.

'And you'll be careful. Drive steady,' she says, turning her face to look at me.

Her cheeks are flared red after her exertions with the snow and a little wisp of hair pokes out from under her woollen hat.

'I'm going to be really careful. Just get there safely, however long it takes, and bring him home.'

'We can't risk leaving him there on his own over Christmas, especially this one,' she tells me but I know she's talking to herself as much as to me. 'Not even at the best of times, but when he's not well ... we have to get him home.'

'We have to get him home,' I echo and in the iced-up car the words have nowhere to go and so they hang until frozen into silence.

Our son Luke is stranded in Sunderland with three days to go to Christmas and Newcastle airport closed. He's at university and living in a rambling, decrepit Edwardian house whose five other students have all decamped for the holidays. So he's on his own and he's not well. What's afflicting him has not been entirely clear from his phone calls but he's got a temperature and symptoms that suggest flu. He's already dragged himself out of his sickbed twice to make the journey to the airport only to find his flight cancelled. Subsequent flights are fully booked and his mother has tormented herself by translating the vague telephone descriptions into things more serious than flu. So perhaps he has pneumonia or, most terrible of all, meningitis. And although she has gone online and then put him over the symptoms like a catechism there is little that can be said to reassure her. Perhaps that's understandable when she has her own insight into the fallibility of the flesh to deal with, and that's another reason to bring him home because he has to be with us at this time, not far away in a world of strangers.

The windscreen is almost cleared. Instinctively I want to squirt water on the remaining fragments of ice but know it will freeze again. We look at each other and she rests her hand on my arm then tells me I'm a good father. It's not a claim I'd ever make for myself but I think that, if I bring our son home, in my own mind it might just help – even tip the balance, however temporarily, in my favour.

'I should be going.'

'I'll get the food and the flasks,' she says and when she opens her door a little seam of snow unravels inside the car. I watch her plod to the kitchen door and suddenly she looks frail inside my hill-walking coat that is several sizes too big for her. She's wearing it over her pyjamas and the pink bottoms froth over the top of her boots. After I'm gone she'll go back to bed and I hope I've left some heat in it for her. I inspect the pile of CDs but can't decide with which one to start the journey.

When Lorna returns I almost smile when I see that she's put everything into the coolbox that is usually reserved for summer picnics. She places it on the passenger seat and straps it in, then takes off the lid to reveal enough provisions to cover every emergency.

'I've put the flask of coffee at the top along with the sandwiches and here are the Lemsips and aspirins,' she says, handing me a plastic bag I recognise from airport security and which is now filled with every medication our home can muster. 'Keep these separate and make sure when you get him that he takes some of the drinks. We need to get his temperature down.' Then she stretches her hand across the seat and I squeeze it gently before she shuts the car door and I start the engine.

It's a Toyota RAV4 and it's never let us down, not once through the eighty thousand miles on the clock, but I listen intently to it in case this might be the first time. It hasn't moved in three days but I've turned the engine over each morning and when it kicks in I pat the steering wheel in gratitude. We cleared the curved driveway down to the gate the previous day so it's bordered by banks of snow and looks like a chicane. I can feel my back grind its own gears as I turn the wheel and understand why clearing snow is a

7

popular precursor to a heart attack. The new fall of snow has been lighter than anything that has gone before so it doesn't represent a problem but I take it slowly, staying in second gear, feeling the way. At the road I pause both to look to see if anything is coming and to do a final inventory of everything I need, patting the inside pocket where the printed boat ticket is, then set my phone in the drink holder beside the handbrake. I can tell from the pristine snow that mine will be the first car on our side road where the jagged hedgerows are momentarily rendered smooth and in the rising light gradually blooming with spangled frost.

I make the left turn and start up the slope – it's not a particularly steep incline but I only get halfway before the wheels spin and the car starts to slip. I put the handbrake on but know I'm not going to make it up, so carefully I let the car roll gently backwards towards our gate. I'm glad Lorna has gone inside and can't see what's happened. There is always a thin rivulet of water running off the field behind the house and down the side of the slope in a narrow tract that some winter mornings reveals itself as black ice. If I am to get traction I need to stay in the middle of the road. For once I wish that some heavy vehicle from one of the surrounding farms has careered along the road and made tracks but the snow only bears witness to my first failed attempt. I try again and almost reach the crest but, when I instinctively press the accelerator to ensure I make the final yards, the car suddenly slithers sideways and then despite everything I do it's sliding slowly down the slope at a crazy angle to the world. Everything is wrong, nothing is in the right place, and I am powerless to affect its trajectory. All my frantic turning of the wheel and pressing of the brakes only seem to exacerbate what is happening and then there is a curious split-second moment of calm, of an almost welcome recognition that this, as you always suspected, is the way the world truly is, and there's nothing for you to do but wait and see what happens.

The car ends up sideways at the bottom of the slope facing the gate it's just exited, as if already admitting failure and seeking to return to its parking spot at the house. It's not a good omen for the journey and I consider abandoning it before it's really even begun but I think of our son and know I can't let him down, can't walk back into the house five minutes after setting out as if I'm giving up without really trying. I hunch over the wheel and then understand that I can't get up the slope from a standing start. Getting turned isn't easy because there isn't much room and when reversing I bump the hedgerow and in the mirror watch as a small flurry cascades against the car's rear glass. But eventually I manage it and head along the flat stretch of road that leads in the opposite direction to the one I want to go until I reach the entrance to a neighbouring house and am able to turn once more. Keeping the car in second gear I build up more speed than I have been able to do before and, taking the slope at a steady pace, avoid touching the brakes. I've made it and the rest of the road that will lead me out to the main one is passable with care. There are more snowmen in front gardens and in my euphoria at surmounting this first obstacle it feels for a second as if they are forming a guard of honour, their black coal eyes fastened on me, wishing me well. I turn on the radio and catch the weather forecast. The voice says that more snow is likely but this time it's the turn of the south of England and ends by issuing warnings against making any but essential journeys.

There is no journey more essential, I inform the voice, than bringing your son home, bringing your sick son home for Christmas, and then as I reach the main road and find it ploughed and gritted I pat the steering wheel once again and switch the radio to the first CD, then tell myself that ghosts leave no prints in the snow.

Music is important in our house and its absence in the last few months has been as dark a marker as anything else. So I'm glad in the privacy of the car I can play it once more without feeling insensitive. Lorna loves Motown and female singers like Dusty Springfield and Adele. And music has been one of the places that Luke and I have been able to come together. We've even been to a couple of concerts – Neil Young in Dublin and The Gaslight Anthem in the Limelight. I felt a bit old in the Limelight but the music was good and no one seemed to mind my presence or make me feel like the oldest swinger in town. In the car I have the music I've chosen for the long hours that stretch ahead – Robert Wyatt, Van Morrison, REM, John Martyn, Nick Cave.

I've also got the Great Lake Swimmers that Luke gave me for my birthday. I've made a point of bringing some that I know Luke likes as well that we can play on the homeward journey – Ash, The Smiths, The National, Neil Young's *On the Beach*. Luke's always played the guitar and in school had a little group on the go until they all went their separate ways to university.

Because it's early and the schools are on holiday the roads are mostly clear of traffic and I make good time. As I enter the city it feels like it's still shut in a slumber, not quite ready to face the day or shrug off the frozen covering that's settled during the night. The Christmas decorations are not yet switched on and the snow is coloured only by the lights of the few cars I meet and the lit foyers of those buildings in which early-morning workers have already started their day. The city looks like one of its sleeping homeless, huddled against the cold and layered in borrowed clothes.

At the docks it seems impossible for the boat to take the number of trucks that are being loaded. One after another they disappear into the bowels of the cargo deck, the air frazzled and momentarily chivvied by their exhausts. A late driver comes scuttling towards his cab with a paper under his arm and a takeaway tea or coffee in the other, hauls himself inside and cracks the engine into noisy life, the folded paper flung against the windscreen. I realise that such journeys are part of a daily ritual of commerce I know nothing about and almost experience a sense of intrusion as I wait in the queue.

As well as the cars and trucks there is a long line of foot passengers I presume are heading home via boat and train now that the airports have let them down. Going home to their families. I wonder how everyone is going to get on, whether my ticket actually guarantees me a place, or is it similar to the way airlines regularly overbook in the belief that a number of their prospective passengers aren't likely to turn up. But before long I'm driving up the ramp, directed into a parking place, and when I get out there is a smell that is instantly recognisable – a mixture of diesel, brine-washed metal and some ingredient to which I can't give a name. Many of the cars I sidle past still have snow on them and in some back seats are carrier bags with presents wrapped in Christmas paper. Following other drivers I climb the stairs and heads towards a passenger lounge.

I remember making the crossing as a child when it felt you were on something akin to a cattle boat. Now it's got a certain plushness and comfort with shops and restaurants, soft seats instead of torn plastic and hard benches. There's even a Christmas tree and piped carols. And I'm being greeted by staff as if I've just walked into a hotel, with the earlier smells replaced by those of food and coffee. The lounge however is already filling up with people using their bags to stake territorial claims, hot drinks in one hand, phones in the other, informing their listeners that they're on the boat, that they're coming home. I send a text to Lorna letting her know that I've made it and the roads weren't too bad.

The young woman on the seat beside me asks if I'll watch her bag while she gets something to eat. When she comes back with a sandwich and coffee I tell her that I'm going to Sunderland to bring my son home. I've already told the woman at the kiosk in the car park who checked my ticket. Maybe it makes me feel good, that I'm doing something mildly heroic, and as someone who spends his life taking photographs of things that don't particularly interest him, there isn't much opportunity to feel heroic. Because what I do is weddings mostly – photos but never a video no matter how much they pay – family portraits, special birthdays, school formals, sometimes a bit of corporate work if I'm lucky and whatever else comes my way.

'He's at Sunderland University and he's not well,' I tell her. 'Airport's closed. His mother has sent me to bring him home.'

'What's he do at uni?' she asks in a Scottish accent.

'Video and film production.'

'I did something like that.'

'In Sunderland?'

'No, in Glasgow. That's where I'm going home to. Hopefully the train's still running.'

'I'd give you a lift if I was going that way,' I say, 'but I'm going to Sunderland,' and then feel as if I'm being too forward and she might think something bad about me. She answers a text and I pretend to look at my own phone.

'What's wrong with your son?'

'We're not sure exactly but it sounds like some kind of flu. Were you visiting Northern Ireland?'

'I work on *Game of Thrones*.'

'That sounds exciting,' I say. I've never seen it but like everybody else know how popular it is even though somewhere lodged in my memory is someone's description of it as 'tits and dragons'.

'It has its moments.'

'My son watches it. Though probably illegally, I guess. Streams most everything.'

'Who doesn't?'

'I laughed when I heard the council had painted white lines down the road with the Dark Hedges.'

'They had to burn the paint off again but you can still see the marks.'

'And what are the actors like?' I ask.

'Mostly pretty cool. Some can be a pain in the ass. Needing this, needing that. Never satisfied.'

'And what do you do?'

'I'm a production assistant,' she says then looks at her phone again and I sense the conversation's over so I don't ask what that entails although meeting her will give me something to tell Luke about on the journey home. And it would be good if I could ask some questions about how she got started.

The boat moves off and I start to watch our progress through the window. The sea is calm, seemingly indifferent to the weather's dramatics, but the snow-covered shoreline that reaches out like two outstretched arms funnelling us to the open sea presents a vista I've never seen before and I think I shouldn't have left the camera in the car. There are some safety announcements and then more of the piped Christmas music. I think of Lorna trying to refind warmth in our bed, of Lilly asleep under her film poster of *The BFG*, Luke far away and alone in an empty house. And suddenly everything feels intensely strange as the present slips into the silent place where memory and consciousness filter into each other to make something new. So for just a few seconds I'm mindful of all the other people who've made this same journey and the passengers around me are replaced by a silent collage of the blurred faces of those who have gone before, many of them looking for new lives in cities that they hoped offered a better future. Of all the women carrying sadness in their wombs forced to seek help far from family and home. I try to blink them away but just as I do I catch a glimpse of a young man on the other side of the lounge before he disappears and I think it's Daniel.

I'm not surprised he's on the boat because I glimpse him in many places, always fleetingly and never long enough for me to raise my hand and call out to him.

Sometimes he's on the end of a line of groomsmen decked out in their hired suits and trying to look like they've stepped out of *Reservoir Dogs*. Other times I catch

him in the corner of my eye when I'm driving, and sometimes just before sleep he's there but always at a distance and I wonder should I get up and check the door
is unbarred so, if he wants, he can come home. I think
I probably see him on the line of groomsmen because
when he was in school and they were getting one of those
panoramic photographs done he and his mate Robbie ran
from their places in the tiered ranks to join the other end
and so appeared twice. The head wasn't amused and he
copped the first of his suspensions. Suspended for being
a joker. Probably his best and least deserved one. There
is the musical chink and whine of a slot machine. We're
slowly heading out to open sea.

I doze a little – all that snow clearing and the early start.
When I wake the young woman has gone and I hope to
hell I wasn't snoring in her ear or she thought I was trying to pick her up. The crossing will only take a couple
of hours but my head already feels fogged and I know I
need it clear if I'm going to make the drive so I go outside and up to the top deck, let the morning air shock me
awake. A group of smokers, some of them with the hoods
of their parkas pulled up, hunch over a railing in the designated smoking area. I see the young woman I was sitting
beside. Wind streams her hair and she has to push it back
from her face. The wake of the boat tumbles and froths
in a V-shape almost like we're churning snow, but the sea
itself as it stretches out beyond seems almost stalled in a
grey torpor. There isn't a feature that would make a photograph even if I had my camera; however there are lots of
people taking selfies, either on their own or as a couple.
The camera phone and the unrelenting progress of technology and everything coming after it are what will kill

off the jobs of people like me. Soon all social photography will be self-done in this way. It sometimes makes me feel like the last of a dying breed. Last of the Mohicans, taking pictures with an actual camera, and it makes it worse to know that however good the technology employed, these pictures of self are in my mind mostly worthless, devoid of whatever it is that makes a proper photograph – one that springs from thoughtful creative decisions and a particular way of seeing. So in my eyes they're not much more than an indulgence, expressions of human vanity and devoid of the dignity that the right photograph can bestow. But if Lilly's right, maybe I really am the 'fun sponge' she's called me and I'm railing against something that's just a bit of harmless pleasure.

We're walking round the cliff path in Portstewart. Tire the boys out even though it was cold then too, almost as cold as it is now. Luke in his constant question phase:

'Why do they call it the seaside?'

'Because we're here at the side of the sea.'

'But why do they call it the seaside?'

'What do you mean, Luke?'

'Why do they call it the side of the sea?'

'What else would you call it?'

'They call it the seaside but how do you know it's the side of the sea and not the front or the back?'

He looks up at me and there's little smudges of brown in the corners of his mouth from where he had a chocolate ice cream in Morelli's. I don't know the answers any more to most of his questions so often I simply say, 'I don't know,' or, 'Just because they do.' Fathers should know the answers to the questions their young sons ask but his come from a different planet so far out in space that it's no longer part of the solar system. So as a distraction I say, 'Look, there's a man fishing.' But the information contains no sense of revelation or enlightenment and so he ignores it and instead concentrates on kicking a stone on to the rocks below. 'You'll scuff your shoes,' I tell him which allows us to feel like father and son again.

I think of him in that strange house, a house with empty rooms, and how terrible that must seem to him. Everyone gone, all the normal sounds of student life collapsed into silence as if the falls of snow have smothered them and in their place only the building's assertion of ownership, with its inexplicable stretches and strains, of the snow pressing down on the roof. Pressing down like the cold weight of loneliness.

Passing voices in the street. His mother's phone calls. Constantly checking online with the airport to see if planes are flying. His packed bag at the foot of the bed. And everything stalled — his flight home, his health, whatever he wants for himself. What does he want for himself? Making films sounds like a careers pitch from *Fantasy Island* but maybe if he gets lucky he might find a role in some organisation that offers more than short-term contracts and menial tasks. We were just so pleased he wanted to go to university we didn't try to interfere with his choice of course and excused ourselves by telling each other that it was important he studied something he was interested in.

Gulls hover a short way from the boat, hanging weightless on the currents. And Luke never seemed to allow himself to be hobbled by anything, casual in his approach to everything, curiously indifferent to any form of pressure that the school or we might try to assert. But maybe that's a good thing. Not to be intense, not to be single-mindedly in pursuit of anything particularly if that thing seems permanently just out of reach. Not to have a hole inside, some kind of void that needs to be filled. Healthy and happy, that's all that matters, we've told ourselves and I still think that was right. I look at the gulls again. We've bought him a drone for Christmas – not one of those massively expensive ones but one that's really not much more than a toy. Still, it has its own inbuilt camera so he'll be able to film things. We've even bought extra batteries.

I don't notice her approach. Her hair is tousled and windblown. I can smell the smoke of her cigarette.

'A bit stuffy inside,' she says and for the first time I register she has eyes that are the grey-green colour of the sea.

'It's cold,' I say.

'When you're a smoker you get used to it. We're the new outcasts. The exiled. Sometimes if you're lucky you get a patio heater.'

'Not here, though.'

'What's Sunderland like?'

'The truth?'

She nods and shifts slightly on her feet as the boat momentarily seems to lurch a little for no obvious reason.

'Some of it's OK, other bits are like Belfast in a bad year on a bad day.'

'I like Belfast. Mostly.'

'I like it now too but the Belfast you like is not the same one as I knew growing up – which is a good thing. Didn't one of those *Game of Thrones* executives slag it off?'

'He said something like it wasn't the most cosmopolitan city to spend half the year in.' She laughs, then adds, 'He had to do a bit of a grovelling apology.'

'Never apologise for the truth,' I tell her before I realise I've said it and it feels a bit like I've made myself her parent. There is a pause in which we both look out at the sea and then I say, 'I was going to ask you about getting started in the business, advice for my son.'

'The honest answer is that I would advise him to do something else. Something that will pay him a decent wage and offer him decent prospects.'

'But you've done well for yourself, haven't you?'

'On *Game of Thrones* I'm only a runner.'

'And what does a runner do?'

'Run here, run there.' It sounds like her standard explanation. 'Run errands. Do everything that there's no one else to do. And you make a lot of tea, carry a lot of things from A to B.'

'But it's a start,' I tell her. 'Perhaps opportunities will open up. And it must be exciting to see the actors and the ...' I struggle for the word and then say 'action'.

'Sometimes, but we're not part of the inner circle and there's a lot of rules and stuff you have to sign up to and if you break any of them the sky falls on you.'

'Or you get fed to a dragon.'

'That's about it,' she says and then wishes me good luck in bringing my son home and I haven't said much more than thanks when she turns and walks away. I never see her again. And afterwards I think that if I knew her name I could have looked for it on the screen credits.

Their presents are in the living room — we never trust putting them in their bedrooms or for them to sleep right through because they'd start the unwrapping without us and rob us of the pleasure of seeing the excitement on their faces and because Lorna expects me to take some photographs when the riot of tearing and squealing begins. But of course they wake early and they're shouting in from their rooms asking is it time yet and we tell them no, to go back to sleep, but it's always useless and so even before the first light we give up all ideas of our own sleep and call them into us. They clamber and bounce on the bed, reluctantly snuggle down, feeling their parents' embraces like straitjackets. Then we play our traditional games, piping up a little duet.

'Well, Mum, do you think Santa's come?'

'Did anyone hear anything during the night?'

'I think I heard something on the roof,' Luke says.

'It was probably that pigeon that's nesting somewhere close and which drives your mother mad with its early-morning cooing.'

'If I had a gun I think I'd shoot it,' Lorna says.

'That would be cruel.'

'Not as cruel as waking your mum and dad up at the crack of dawn.'

'Can we go and look now? Please, please, please.'

'Soon, very soon,' I say as I put my hand lightly across his eyes. 'Why don't you both take a snooze so that you won't be done in before the day's over?'

'No, no,' they squeal and they're squirming so much the duvet is sliding off the bed.

'OK, OK. Take it easy. But first of all an important question. Have you both been good?'

They answer yes without the slightest hesitation and I look at Lorna and ask her what she thinks. She ponders it for a moment, her finger across her lips in an exaggerated pose of thinking deeply, keeping them waiting.

'Mostly I would say ... mostly I would say yes! Now go to your rooms and put on your dressing gowns and slippers and then come back in here until your dad turns on some lights and the heating.'

I put on my own dressing gown and slippers, lift the camera whose battery I've charged during the night and head to the kitchen where the smell of the preparations for the meal we are going to share still lingers. The heating kicks itself unenthusiastically into life and then I go into the living room, switch on the Christmas-tree lights and the picture ones so the light is soft. They have Christmas sacks under the tree that have the smaller stocking fillers – sweets, balsawood planes, card games, football socks, shin pads, chocolate money, tiny torches. Their main presents are arranged at opposite ends of the settee. Lorna's good at wrapping and the piles look like little pyramids with the largest to the bottom.

'Can we come in yet?' they shout. 'Can we come?'

'Just one second more when I call you.'

And each year I take the photograph of this perfect moment before it shatters.

It feels like the start of a race. We're all revving up and ready to go. There aren't that many cars on board compared to the number of lorries. It's just over a hundred miles to Carlisle so in normal conditions this part of the journey should take about two hours. I have made it three times. The first with Lorna when we delivered Luke as a fresher, the car packed to the gills with everything he might need to survive in student halls, the second time

21

when I brought all his stuff home because after first year he had to move out of the halls, and then at the start of his second year took him and all of his belongings back again. So the route is reasonably familiar to me but when I leave the port the snow has rebranded everything changed and the places that linger in my memory are wiped clean.

Turn right on to London Road. Stay on the A75. The road out of Stranraer is improved from how it used to be decades earlier. But now it's narrowed with clunky piles of cleared snow pushed to each side and although the surface seems mostly clear it still looks shiny with danger and I keep my speed down, hunker behind the wheel and try to shut out everything but the music and feel the reassuring familiarity of the mechanical, of what responds to anything I want it to do.

It's a woman's voice giving the directions. I'm used to women's voices. Sometimes they're keen to talk. Maybe there's stuff they need to say before they walk down the aisle.

'I don't know if I'm doing the right thing,' she says as she holds her hands out for her nail polish to dry and she's looking at me as if I'm the person who knows the answer.

'Only you know that,' I tell her because I've been here before and it seems like the best thing to say.

The make-up girl has gone and there's just the two of us. And more and more I'm there in situations like this because the fashion's changed and no one wants a series of stiffly formal photographs any longer. They want these quirky, arty shots as well as the happy couple and in-laws. They've also started to want photos that aren't taken on church steps or in hotel gardens. So now I have to be prepared to take shots on beaches, in the ruins of castles or in one case a stable. The last shot was her sitting on a horse, him holding the bridle, like the winning jockey being led in. Anywhere the happy couple wants. Anywhere they want. But now I'm not sure there is a happy couple.

'You're bound to be nervous,' I tell her then take a picture of her footwear that she hasn't put on yet, arrange the white sparkly shoes that look like they've been made from icing sugar and her hand-held posy of pink roses on a cushion for another shot. She's sitting at her dressing table looking at herself in the mirror. If I can keep myself out of the photograph I can take a shot of her looking at her reflection. Her mother is calling her to get a move on. She faces herself in the mirror with her hands stretched out and I don't know whether she's inviting herself into what's ahead or if she's holding it off.

'I met him on a dating site,' she says and just for a second when I glance at her, her outstretched hands make it look like she's sleepwalking. Sleepwalking with her eyes open.

'Lots of people do that now,' I say and I know it doesn't sound good but it's running across my mind that if she backs out now the chances of me getting paid aren't great. Wedding no-shows leave nothing but chaos in their wake. 'As good as anywhere else,' I tell her. 'And the sun's out,' I say as I go to stand at the bedroom window. Down below the wedding car is sitting at the pavement, light puddling in its polished blackness. Her mother calls again. 'Listen; let me take one last photo of you sitting there. You look great. I can catch your reflection in the mirror so it'll come out really well.'

She looks at her nails for a last time before dropping her hands to her side and angles herself to the camera. But the first thing I see is myself in the glass and in that second before I move out of range I want to tell her that I can't help because I can't help myself any more and no matter what she decides it will only ever hold a promise, not any permanent assurance. And one of the few things I know for sure now is that nothing comes with a guarantee. But the only thing I say is, 'Got it.'

She takes one last look at herself and I hear her say with a lilt, 'Bring it on,' and I don't know if the music I'm hearing in her voice is happy or sad but I too say, 'Bring it on,' and try to make my voice echo hers.

At the roundabout take the second exit and stay on the A75. Keep straight ahead. I tell her that's exactly what I intend to do. So yes, bring it on – the miles of snow-seamed roads unwinding to that empty house in Sunderland. To my left the hills and woods look mysterious and still. Most of the side roads I pass remain uncleared, some with only a narrow single track cut through the snow like someone has sliced through a wedding cake. I'm keeping my speed about or slightly under forty miles an hour which is going to make the journey longer but hopefully lessens the chances of disaster. And at intervals along the side of the road are vehicles that look like they have been abandoned and not yet recovered by their owners. I wonder where they found refuge when the worst of the snow hit. I need to stop to phone Luke to tell him that I'm coming and to take the leak I should have taken on the boat but there isn't anywhere obvious because I pass lay-bys that are blocked with several feet of snow so I have to keep going. After about twenty more minutes I see, as if in a miracle, a partially cleared lay-by complete with a van selling hot food and a couple of parked-up lorries. When I turn carefully into it she's telling me that she's recalculating and the screen starts rebooting. I tell her to relax but she doesn't listen, in a tizzy until I silence her. The van is blazoned with the name The Jolly Friar and its owner is wearing a white apron, a woolly hat and a scarf so long that it must be a health and safety risk any time he goes near the fryer. On his hands are fingerless gloves. Fairy lights circle the serving counter and a plastic Merry Christmas banner that looks as if it's seen several years' service is pinned below. A couple of lorry drivers are standing to one side eating burgers so big they're using both hands, their heads jerking forward like pigeons each time they take a mouthful. The smell of cooked onions curdles the air but I've no stomach for such things at this time of the morning and order a coffee, thinking it best to keep the flask's contents until later or an emergency. Despite the name on the van the guy serving is pretty dour and I regret telling him that I'm going to get my son because it elicits no response other than an almost imperceptible nod and he looks at the coins I've given him as if he suspects they might be counterfeit.

Maybe business is bad, smacked in the gob by the snow. Maybe he was hoping to mint it big before the expense of Christmas. I try one last time.

'You did well getting out and about today,' I tell him.

'Not expecting much business but every little bit helps keep the wolf from the door,' he says as he rubs a cloth over the countertop without looking at me. 'Wasn't even supposed to be my turn but the son's buggered off to Aviemore.'

'For the skiing?'

'Aye, the skiing and the getting banjaxed.'

'Bad combination, skiing and drinking.'

'He's up early on the slopes whatever the night before. Says the cold clears the head. A good fry-up does it for me — no need to hurtle down any mountain.'

I wish him good luck and want him to wish me it in return but he simply nods. I slip behind some trees near a couple of picnic tables and as I'm going I look up at the thick cluster of trees that stretches upward into the shadowed distance. Everything is silent and still and the deeper my eyes journey into the wood the deeper the silence and stillness. Even a small bird fretting a fine mist of falling snow doesn't break the spell. If I had my camera I would take a photograph but wonder if I could even get close to capturing what is hidden in the moment. And I hear a voice, my personal satnav, telling me that despite all those hopes I harbour and have always harboured about what I could do and be with the camera, I'm not up to it. And its voice becomes my voice and it's saying over and over, 'Look this way please. Everyone smiling.' Everyone always pretending to smile. I suddenly shiver.

Something brushes a branch further up the slope and snow falls almost in slow motion. I know it's Daniel even though I can't see him. Standing perfectly still I stare and stare, trying to see him, but there are no prints in the snow only the white bark of the birch trees passing coldness to each other.

'Hi, Luke, how are you now? I'm on my way.'

'That's good. How are the roads?'

'Not so bad at the moment. Doable and I'm being careful. So how are you feeling?'

'A bit better but still pretty ropey.'

'And are you drinking plenty?'

'Yes, Dad.' His voice is that of the exasperated teenager. There's a pause and then he says, 'It's the first time you've ever encouraged my drinking.'

'Very funny,' I say, glad that he's well enough to make a joke. 'And you'll be packed so we can do a quick turn-around and head back up here so we get a sailing home.'

'I'm packed now. Ready to leave.'

'OK, I'll let you go and I'll ring when I'm almost there.'

'Dad, can you ask Mum to stop phoning me every five minutes. It's doing my head in and she rings when I'm try-ing to sleep.'

'She's worried about you, Luke, but I'll tell her. Any problems, you ring us. OK?'

'OK,' he says and then he's gone.

I call Lorna and try to do it as gently as possible but she gives out to me because it's only natural that she's worried and she wants to keep tabs on how he is and whether they need to phone for a doctor. She goes silent, which is always worse, until I hear her say that she'll not ring until after lunch then asks me if I've eaten anything yet. I tell her yes and then end the call but what I'm thinking is, there has to be a way of loving your child that gets it right, helps them in whatever way they need but doesn't do their heads in. Don't know how you find that way. Happy families. Everybody smiling. Perfect little groupings – sometimes in their homes, sometimes in the studio, the children all shiny faced and well-off healthy. Sometimes they think black and white will make it classier, lend it an air of gravitas, per-manence even. So who gets ownership of it if there's a divorce? And when the children look back on it what do they see and how much does it match up to their mem-ories? I have two photos to remind me. Both are black and white. Simple snapshots. Both with my mother. One in Santa's Grotto taken in a Belfast city-centre store and one on a first bicycle. No sign of my father.

Luke was never much into drinking. Got himself bladdered the night his GCSE exams finished. That was about the sum total of his teenage excess, at least as far as we know. One of his friends called me on Luke's phone and I went to collect him at the locked back gates of a local park. Propped up by his friend who at least had the good grace to call and not do a runner, a surf of empty WKD bottles round their feet and from somewhere deeper in the park loud shouts and sounds of revelry. Getting him over the gate was one of the most physically difficult things I've ever had to do with Luke. Getting him over a high and locked metal gate. 'Put your foot there, Luke.' Pushing and hauling – I'd never touched my son so much since he was a child and remember how strange it felt. 'Now haul your left leg over.' Trying to stop him breaking his neck, Luke losing one of his trainers in the process. Walking him.

Telling him, 'You're not getting in the car if you're going to hoop.' His hooping as if on demand. Then, when he was finished, hooping again until finally there was nothing left. Walking him some more, trying to sort him so his mother didn't see him in that state.

We got off light with Luke – I know that now. And perhaps as a kind of an apology for the drinking night he turned up at the studio on results day with his list of successes. I didn't hug him because we don't really go in for that and probably haven't touched him since that night at the locked gate but I did something that, if anything, felt more intimate – I took his picture. Sat on a stool, the piece of paper in his hand, I took my son's portrait. And as

I looked at him through the lens I remember that I didn't want the moment to end, didn't want to press the button. Just wanted to hold the moment there with him looking happy and me feeling proud. And wanting to say something but not knowing exactly what it was or how to say it so instead I took him out and we had a Subway.

Strange names on the signs – Wigtown, Gatehouse of Fleet, Kirkcudbright. *Stay on the A75. Then take the second exit at the next roundabout.* My photo with my mother in Santa's Grotto. It was either in Robinson & Cleaver's or Anderson & McAuley's, one of those old-fashioned Edwardian-style family stores that the new multinationals modernised out of existence. I don't remember which one it was. Possibly the last time I enjoyed Christmas. Now, the word grotto seems not a world away from ghetto and that's what it mostly feels like, shut in with high-walled predetermined expectations that never quite get delivered. Going so stir crazy you eventually escape only to end up walking round sales even though you've had a surfeit of stores and the gap between Christmas and the shops demanding more of your money is about five minutes and getting shorter every year. Our local garage was even open on Christmas morning. This year Lorna's job in primary school as a classroom assistant didn't finish until yesterday and I needed to be the one doing the running, getting everything in, ticking off the lists and then being handed new lists. And Lorna needs to rest up, build up her strength, and if I can bring Luke safely home that'll be one less thing for her to worry about. This will be the first Christmas so it won't always be easy but we've talked about it and we've got to pull it off for Lilly, who's still young enough to get excited and entitled to have her expectations realised as best we can.

The satnav goes curiously quiet but just as I'm wondering if she's taking a coffee break she tells me once more *Stay on the A75. Drive for five point four miles.* I pass houses set back from the road that are temporarily transformed into Swiss chalets, only the presence of brick rather than wood confounding the impression. Some gardens have snowmen – snowmen waiting to fly through the air when everyone is sleeping. Luke always slept through the night a short time after he was born. At first a kind of mellow child mostly, then intensely curious about the world and when he'd exhausted his questions, outwardly at least, seemed willing to accept that was just the way it was, that there weren't always answers to what he asked. But there is one question I'd like to ask him and it's what goes on inside his head because I've never had any real insight into that and he rarely says or does stuff that gives you clues. After what's happened that's something more for me to worry about. You'd think that when you were the father of a child, a child you've brought up – well in the sense you were there when they were growing up, because I've come to believe that it's mostly life itself that brings them up – that this would enable your understanding of them, that there would be an instinctive connection between you. *At the next roundabout take the second exit.* How many bloody roundabouts are there? But it doesn't seem to work like this. And I think of my own father as I've started to do more often in recent days and perhaps I'm looking back trying to find whatever connection might have existed before it went missing.

My hands splayed on the wheel. Large, broad-fingered copies of his. But his were useful in the work he did – a small-time jobbing builder who stumbled from one job to another to make a living and whose talk of making a killing was always linked to some final payday far in the future. A killing that never came before Parkinson's cut him down, these strong, calloused hands shaking like the last of winter's windblown leaves into a final helplessness. Mine are a hindrance, not well suited for pressing small buttons and anything that needs a delicacy of touch. A wind is picking up, breathing fine sifts of snow off the tops of walls and the roofs of cars. The branches of a row of fir trees have become a latticed framework of white. It was winter when I helped him work on Old Man Dobson's place out on the Peninsula where the wind snarled off the Lough and sawed at our bones. I was sixteen, conscripted in the holidays, and sometimes I thought I'd be blown off the scaffolding while working on one of the gables. Dobson driving out every afternoon in his blue Merc and humiliating my father for some fault or other and when the job was done quibbling over the final payment and wanting money off for some supposedly slipshod piece of work. My father telling me as we drove home that with any luck some stormy night when the wind roared in off the sea it would take the whole bloody roof off and leave Dobson shivering under the stars. He wanted to erase the pain of the humiliation that I had witnessed and, although I said nothing much, I wanted to let him know that I was on his side so I told him everyone knew that Dobson was a tosser. It was the closest I ever felt to him. There was never a time in the subsequent years when he expressed anything as personal to me, or me to him. As a thin sleet of snow thrown from a passing lorry skims the windscreen I hear a voice say that maybe it's only in the modern world that everyone thinks words are important. But in the following years it felt that the space between us grew slowly wider and then there's no way back and it's pretty sad and all too late. So I suddenly understand that biology and genes don't actually bestow a connection, that whatever finally exists is only through what has been made with these same hands that grip the wheel and not just by a name on a birth certificate. And I want to ring Luke and tell him that I love him but can't because he'll think that I'm the one who's ill, that I'm burning up with some fever.

'And did you ever tell me that you loved me?' Daniel asks.

He comes silently so I never know the time and place but on this journey I've been waiting for him – I can't be alone in the car for all these hours without him coming, despite the hoped-for protection from the music, despite the voice of the satnav. It's often when I'm thinking of Luke that he comes. He's wearing his black hoody with the hood up but it can't stop me registering the pallor of his skin, the dark circles under his eyes. It's those eyes I always look at most because they alone are able to reveal the truth.

'If I didn't tell you, I showed you every day and your mother must have told you so often you can't have heard her any more.'

'But it wasn't true. It was never true, was it?'

'You're full of shit, Daniel.'

'You know it's true,' he insists as he turns his face away from me and stares out through the glass and the light of the snow streams through him. His hands are tightened into fists that clutch his jeans. His right hand has a scab. There is a hole that looks like a cigarette burn in his sleeve.

'You'd like it to be true because then you'd have someone to blame, someone other than yourself.'

I can't take his blame, can't take it any more, because if I do it'll beat me down so low that I'll never be able to get up. But I have to try and talk to him. Try to explain.

That's all that's left to me now.

'How you keeping?' I ask, all the anger deliberately pushed from my voice.

'I'm good, doing good,' he says but the lies are in his eyes. 'Doing even better if I could borrow some money. A little would do.'

'You know I've got no money for you, big or small.'

'Some love.'

I go to tell him that if I didn't love him I'd give him the money, give him whatever he asked, but he's already gone and all I can do is hold the steering wheel a little tighter, turn the music up louder. 'You're full of shit,' I tell him again even though he's no longer there and without realising it I'm shouting. 'Full of shit.' And I slam the steering wheel with the palms of my hands then jump when I accidentally hit the horn. A few seconds later my phone rings. It's Lilly and even though I shouldn't I've answered it because a phone call could mean anything and I try to calm myself.

'Hi, Dad, are you nearly there yet?'

'I'm still in Scotland but I'm getting there. Is Mum all right?'

'Yes. She's lighting a fire in the front room. We're going to toast marshmallows.'

'She knows we're not supposed to because we live in a clean-air zone.'

'But it's Christmas.'

'It doesn't matter.'

'Knock knock.'

'Who's there?'

'Snow.'

'Snow who?'

'Snow skating because the ice is too thin.'

'Very good. And you look after your mum. Don't let her do too much. I have to go now. Back soon.'

'Bye, Dad.'

A surprise child. Out of the blue. A source of pleasure now but I don't want to think about the future. I try not to think of it either when I have to take the pregnant shoots that some mothers-to-be now want because it seems scans aren't record enough any more and thanks to Demi Moore they think it's the thing to do. Some of them even bring a photocopy of the magazine cover where she's standing with one hand supporting her fullness and the other covering her breasts. I always insist they bring their partner with them or a friend because I'm taking no chances of a misunderstanding and I do them as quickly and as tastefully as possible because any hanging around makes me feel uncomfortable, a voyeur rather than a photographer, and sometimes their hand isn't big enough to cover what needs covered so then I have to suggest a type of drape. And there's always photoshopping involved because none of us looks like Demi Moore when we're in the buff. And it's a bit delicate sometimes because I have to ask, 'Do you want your tattoo in the shot?' Mostly they disappoint me by saying yes and I feel obliged to lie that their butterfly, rose or dolphin looks like the business, rather than some crayon drawing Lilly did when she was four.

But what it's like to carry a child inside you for nine months and how that affects the way you think of them for the rest of your life is something I can't ever know because I'm a man and all I've contributed was when the moment's desire expelled a million sperm and all I've done is buy a conception lottery ticket, let nature pick the winning number. Some of the mothers-to-be are embarrassed when the moment comes but others are flirtatious and when they remove the dressing gown that I've asked them to bring and get them to wear while we work out positions, sort out lighting, they do it with a theatrical flourish as if they're on set. I always feel obliged to say something to hide the fact that I'm usually the one who's embarrassed and so I generally use 'Looks good. Hold it there' because it suggests I'm talking of the photo's composition but leaving the possibility that it might include them as well.

I hit a part of the road where for some reason less snow seems to have been cleared so the traffic slows to a crawl for a couple of miles. The car is stuffy and I open my window and feel the rush of cold air against my face. Thirty seconds later I close it again and eat one of the sandwiches Lorna has made. Then the traffic starts to pick up speed and before long I find myself with a lorry in front and a lorry behind that's too close which feels like it's impatient, pressurising me to go faster than I feel is safe. I'm glancing constantly in my mirror but can't see the driver and suddenly it seems as if I'm in that Spielberg film *Duel* only this time we're not in a Californian desert but in a winter landscape that's underwritten with treachery and I think if the lorry in front comes to a sudden halt I don't have braking distance and I could end up sandwiched between two forty-tonne vehicles. Starting to get television images in my head of those crashes which so disturbingly undermine your belief in the supposed strength of metal, I look for a turn-off, but nothing offers a safe escape and so for another couple of miles I reluctantly stay in convoy trying to gradually lower my speed to create more distance between me and the lorry in front. The one behind feels so physically close that I think if I have to stop suddenly it would simply roll over the top of me. And suddenly it's not *Duel* I'm driving in but *Ice Road Truckers* with its hale and hearty drivers, talking up the danger, all fired-up on their private image of themselves as the Pony Express delivering the mail across distant and dangerous frontiers. I watch late at night when the house is silently sleeping and the stop-start hum from the fridge, the wallop of weary hot-water pipes, transmutes into the groan of the ice as I imagine the fissures spreading like lightning forks. All that weight of truck and cargo plunging into the lake's dark waters and I read enough books to understand that it's a metaphor for all our journeys. Before I go to bed I look in at Lilly, let the sound of her breathing seep through me until I'm washed clean, feel a new steadiness in my silent steps. And when I sleep I try not to have that recurring dream where I'm walking out across a frozen lake. Further and further.

Waiting for the sudden crack. Sometimes seeing a face I recognise below the ice.

When people tailgate me I feel the temptation to hit the brakes, let them learn their lesson, but of course I never do because that's mutually disastrous regardless of who's in the right. *Drive for six point four miles*. More than anything I'd like to be weightless, to walk across whatever ice stretches out ahead and never again to hear that splintering sound. When we were kids we'd break ice puddles, make the ice tear and screech, smash the thicker surfaces with the heels of our wellingtons. A rule-keeping child's timid substitute for breaking windows and perhaps it's my imagination but despite the music playing in the car I've started to become conscious of the slushy sounds coming from below my wheels and know if it freezes again the surface will be like glass. I keep looking for a turn-off road where I can remove myself from a potential disaster but the side roads all look choked with snow and seem to offer limited prospects of a turn back to the right direction. Then just when I'm thinking of flicking on my hazards as a kind of warning to the driver behind, she tells me *At the next roundabout take the second exit* and I understand that this is my best chance so as I enter the roundabout which is laden with a mass of dumped snow I pass on the second exit and do a circle of it to bring me back on the right road, but this time behind the second lorry. And I settle down again to a speed I feel is safer. Safer only on the outside because the after-echo of Daniel still lingers, reluctant to fade back into the music even though it's one of my favourite songs, so I put it on repeat and listen to Van Morrison's 'Snow in San Anselmo', trying to place myself inside the different parts of the story with the waitress telling me snow is coming down for the first time in thirty years; a pancake house that's open twenty-four hours; some madman looking for a fight. The choir, his voice, the moment. Just the moment. But Daniel's voice is a descant over the top of everything and the echo doesn't fade but instead returns to the very instant of its release.

A son so full of shit that it leaches to the surface of his skin and finds expression in pitted blemishes like some piece of bruised fruit. The fruit of my loins, that's what they call your child, so this is to be my life's harvest. This is what has been brought to fruition and as always there's the same question, repeated over and over, as to how you tended that growth, how well you protected it from disease. I tell myself that the world is filled with infected spores, that they blow where they will, carried on currents invisible to the eye and so impossible to repulse. But none of it convinces and I am shackled to that inescapable burden of guilt and, despite knowing I must somehow find a way to glimpse even the beginning of absolution if I am to survive, I don't know how that can be done so all there is for me to do is keep the car on the road, keep covering the miles and bring Luke home.

A sign for Lockerbie. A burning plane falling out of the sky. It makes me shiver. Presumably the landscape is healed with all the signs of devastation long cleared away, replaced by memorials and lives destined never to return to the way they were. I can't be sure but I think it happened on a day close to Christmas. Maybe even as close as this very day. I can't remember either whether it fell into snow before it scorched the earth black. But as I strain to think about it I remember a father whose daughter was on the plane, campaigning to find the truth of what happened and then coming to believe that the man who ended up in prison was not the guilty one. And I've started to wonder if there is always a truth that's given to us so we never discover other, more inconvenient ones. I'm not someone who believes in every conspiracy theory but when you've lived through a period of the Troubles it gradually begins to dawn on you that we've given up on facts. Partly because they're in dispute but mostly because they're deemed unhelpful to a future based on agreement. So now there's only what they call narratives and we're all allowed to have our different ones, even if I think my narrative is the one that's true and yours is make-believe. Anyway, what's it matter because unless you've had someone blown to pieces or their throat cut on account of the road they were walking on – it's a narrative, just another story. Washed up in the wake of our history your story doesn't even belong to you any more – someone else can claim ownership of it, make it part of theirs.

I pass a man on skis, both poles working like pistons as he snow-walks to wherever the hell he's going. I know that I have to hold Daniel's story close, not let anyone else find a different narrative, impose a different reading, because I'm the one who needs to make sense of it. I'm still trying every day, every single day to do that, and perhaps in time, even though I can't easily imagine it, it might become a story that can be shared because I don't need a shrink to tell me that holding it so close will be corrosive and stop me being fully what I need to be for my children. These are things I know in my head but have not yet felt in my heart, or being, or wherever it is you need to experience them.

I'm travelling in a strange land. The world outside the car is snowbound, utterly changed – so much snow that everywhere looks deeply buried. Mostly what I like about driving is that it allows you to drift into an internal cruise control where even mechanical actions are instinctive and largely unregistered, so sometimes you can suddenly look out and momentarily grasp where you are, without having any real memory of how you got there. But now although the snow seems at first to homogenise the world I am sensitive to every vibration of the car and register everything I see as if they are markers guiding the way — a snow-blistered stone wall, a particular shape of tree that looks like it's wearing a wind-shivered wedding dress, road signs that are layered with white. And outside the world of the car there are people missing on mountains, remote villages cut off, farmers getting drops of fodder for their animals. Grounded flights, the country frozen into immobility. My son unable to get home. There's something they're not telling us about the weather. I buy into global warming but I think there's other stuff they're hiding from us. And what I don't understand is why when the world is getting warmer last summer was a washout and why this winter has produced more snow than we can handle. I pass landscapes that seem to beg for a photograph but right now I know that the result would be nothing more than a cheap calendar shot for December. Snow for December, autumn leaves for October and lambs for spring — I did one for a local bank once. That was what they wanted. Not exactly Ansel Adams. Devoid of all mystery. No *Thundercloud, Lake Tahoe*; no *Aspens, Northern New Mexico*; no *Oak Tree*, no *Snowstorm* — the images that are lodged in whatever creative memory I still have left. Landscape living in the eye, transmuting itself until it can only be seen through some dream of the imagination, so that the image is both itself and something new that can't be described in words. And that feels like it's out of my reach because whatever part of me needs to be alive to make it happen is also frozen into immobility.

Children sledge in a field ploughing white furrows behind them. Luke has an eye. I saw that early and tried to encourage it without making a fuss. He did good work for his A-level art portfolio – pictures of old and derelict buildings in Belfast. Getting harder to find them but round North Street and one of the old entries offered opportunities. I went with him, just to drive him and keep an eye on him and did my very best not to get in the way or be the advising voice on his shoulder, because it's one of the paradoxes of parenting that most of the time things work best when space is offered and there's no surer way of sending your children spinning into some far-off orbit than to try and hold them tightly inside your gravitational pull.

He managed to put together a visually interesting collection, focusing on textures and decay, letting the camera find the stories, using shade and light to capture a sense of the city's older materials, sometimes effectively juxtaposing the old and new that exist cheek by jowl. Afterwards he did some photoshopping, some of which I liked and other bits I wasn't so keen on because it seemed to me that the subject matter spoke out loudly for itself and didn't need any tarting up. But it was his call and I saw enough to know that he has a talent so all I can do is encourage him and share any technical knowledge that he might need. But I'll let him do the asking. And what I worry about with Luke is that apart from music he never seems able to stick with one thing for very long. So during his teenage years he's gone through a range of hobbies – judo, cycling, rock climbing, even fencing – but never focused on anything for more than about six months and his wardrobe and our garage are lumbered with the subsequent debris of discarded equipment. His mother has offered to sell his stuff on Gumtree but he seems reluctant to give her the go-ahead even though like all students he could do with the money. Perhaps there is some part of him that believes he might retrace his steps, isn't sure what might be needed and what might not.

There's a garage open and I pull in to top up with petrol because despite my three-quarters-full tank and the small canister in the boot I harbour a paranoia about running out in some wilderness. I also want to call Lorna. They've managed to clear the entrance and exit and access to two pumps. Everywhere has been gritted and outside they have sledges for sale. They're nothing much more than thin red plastic with a string attached at the front but they'll do the business and I decide to buy one for Lilly. We'll have to find a slope somewhere – I think maybe we could go to the grounds at Stormont, put it to some honest use for once.

'Where are you now?' Lorna asks.

'On the way to Gretna Green.'

'Have you found someone to run away with you?'

'I'd be so lucky. Any word from Luke?'

'Haven't spoken to him. In case you've forgotten, I'm not allowed to ring him.'

'Of course you can ring him but maybe not quite so often. If he's in diffs he'll let us know.'

There is silence on the end of the phone just long enough to let me know that I've said something stupid so I try to get back on track by asking how she is.

'So-so. I'm a bit tired. Don't know if it's in my body or in my head. There's always something else to get done before Christmas Day. Something you've forgotten no matter how well organised you think you are.'

'You need to take it easy, not overdo things. No one's going to worry if everything's not perfect.'

Another moment of silence before I hear her irritation say, 'I want it to be perfect. For Lilly and Luke. And if not perfect then as good as we can make it. And I need you to help.'

I start to outline the ways I've already helped – the running around, the completion of multiple lists, two nightmare visits to Smyths toyshop at Forestside, where the atmosphere amongst parents desperate to procure the final must-have craze was at best sharp-elbowed and at worst cut-throat, but she insists, 'That's not what I mean. What I want from you is for you to be there and part of it, not standing on the sidelines and looking for some hiding place until it all blows over. This year more than ever. Do you understand what I'm saying?'

I could say I don't then take defence in simulated confusion but the truth is I fully grasp what it is she means and that knowledge is accompanied by a pulse of shame that my previous efforts have fallen so short.

'Absolutely. I'll be giving it my very best shot. Doing whatever needs to be done.'

'But I don't want you doing that because you have to. I want you to do it for yourself as well as all of us. And Lilly wants to speak to you.'

'Hi, Dad. Are you still in Scotland?'

'Yes, but not for much longer. Are you going to track Santa's journey on the computer like you did last year?'

'I was only nine then.'

'So you're too old now for tracking Santa,' I say, realising that while she's on the cusp of knowing the adult truth, she's still not sure and is hedging her bets.

'Why does Santa come down the chimney?'

'I don't know, Lilly. Why does Santa come down the chimney?'

'Because it suits him. Do you get it?'

'Yes, I get it.'

'But you didn't laugh.'

'I didn't laugh but I'm really smiling, smiling ear to ear. It was a good one.'

I tell her to put her mother back on and we talk for a few more minutes and I try to sound as if I'm bringing back both our son and a new enthusiasm for all that lies ahead. Tell her I won't be a fun sponge. I understand now that we're going to try and fill the spaces that have opened up in our lives with a collective attempt at happiness, that we're to come close together, closer than ever before, and replace our emptiness with festive cheer, and I'm suddenly scared that we won't be able to pull it off, that we'll be papering over the cracks. The house is already awash with decorations, a real tree and outside lights on the front garden's cherry blossom. I had asked if she really wanted those lights up and she had looked at me as if I had just defiled something and never answered a single word so I got them up and switch them on each night so they shine outside our house and link us to all the other houses on our road with their Santa-climbing chimneys, illuminated reindeers and guttering festooned with icicles that blink.

I think it's these lights, ours and those of all the other houses, that are the closest this time comes to retaining any religious impulse. Setting aside the competitive element that drives some, or the desire to say look at me, for most it's the star they're following in the hope that even in the darkness of winter these few days might lead them to somewhere they can rekindle joy. That's what we'll be trying to do but I don't know what the prospects are of success. We're lucky to have Lilly and I want to believe we'll get through by focusing mostly on her.

In the garage entrance my feet crunch on grit the colour of brown sugar. The woman behind the counter is wearing flashing reindeer ears and when she says, 'Desperate weather,' I feel encouraged to tell her that I'm going to Sunderland to bring my son home from uni.

'That's a journey,' she says.

'Has to be done.'

'If you'd been doing it two days ago you'd never have got as far as Carlisle. Nothing was getting through here. But since then they've got most main roads moving again.' Then, when she sees me looking at the newspaper on the counter that's got the headline of WINTER WIPE-OUT, adds, 'Yesterday's news today, or is it today's news yesterday?' She laughs and says, 'Whatever it is, they didn't get here in time. You can take one if you like. No charge.'

I lift one out of politeness and she wishes me good luck on my journey. It feels like a nice thing she's done and I thank her and, going back to the car, move it away from the pump then pour a coffee from the flask and have another sandwich. I throw the paper in the back seat because I know to read it is to fill my head with stuff that runs counter to what you're trying to feel about Christmas. So to make it through the coming days requires you to shut yourself off as best as possible, keep out all the bad things that are fermenting in the world. All the terrors and the tortures, all the detonations of hate. The tsunami of suffering. And I don't know what we're going to do about Daniel. Is he part of our inner world or locked outside? I avoid dwelling on it by telling myself that I need to be going. I'm already behind schedule but still doing all right, all things considered. As I turn towards the exit I see a woman standing there. Even though she's layered in coats and a hat it's obvious that she's not young and she's holding two renewable bags filled with groceries, one of which is emblazoned with a slogan that promises to last a lifetime. As I get closer she waves and I wave back before I realise that she's not waving but trying to hitch a lift. There isn't another car on the forecourt and she knows I've seen her so driving straight past doesn't feel right. I put the window down and ask her where she's going. She comes up close to the window and I can see she's studying me, trying to decide whether I'm an axe murderer or not, so it's only when I pass the test that she tells me, 'Just a couple of miles up on the front of the road.' I lift the coolbox off the passenger seat, squeeze it into the space behind and help her with one of the bags as she clambers in. The seatbelt gets lost in the folds of her coat and I have to search for it then fasten it for her.

'Out doing your shopping,' I say. 'Getting stocked up.'

'Need to get everything in so I don't have to go out again. This is very good of you.'

'No problem.'

'The car wouldn't start so it was walk or starve. But the bags are heavy enough so I thought I'd try to get a lift from some kind soul.'

It makes me feel momentarily good to be thought of as some kind soul. The green wax coat she's wearing looks dried out as if it's been hanging in a cupboard somewhere and there's a slight smell of mildew clinging to it. I lower my window about an inch. She must be in her seventies and when she takes off her gloves the veins on the back of her hands are raised and heavily inked.

'Did you get everything?'

'I think so. It doesn't take much to keep me ticking over. And I got an oil-fill at the start of the month so I'll not go cold.'

'So you're all set for Christmas then.'

'Just another day for me,' she says, but without any trace of self-pity in her voice.

'Are you on your own?'

'Sure I'll have the Queen to keep me company.'

'So you're not an independence voter then.'

'Well, I did vote for it,' she says then adds, 'but company is company.' She rubs the back of her hand with the palm of the other and I turn the heater up, turn the music down that I had forgotten was even on. 'I have a son. He used to work on the oil rigs but now he's out in the Middle East. Sometimes in dangerous places but he says they pay him good money for taking the risk.'

'And he won't be home for Christmas?'

'No, he'll still be out there.'

'Do you Skype him?'

But she doesn't understand what I mean and when I explain she tells me she doesn't have a computer. Then she pulls a mobile phone from her pocket and looks at it as if she's seeing it for the first time.

'He got me this. I don't use it much. It's really for emergencies.'

'Perhaps he'll call you on Christmas Day.'

'Maybe,' she says, but there isn't much conviction in her voice. 'Do you have children?'

I avoid the new and unwelcome complexities of answering that simple question by telling her I have a son at university in Sunderland and I'm going to bring him home.

'I hope I'm not keeping you back,' she says then tells me her house is just a bit further along the main road.

'You're OK,' I say.

We pass a little hamlet of houses and a school that has already shed its children and staff. The windows are a blizzard of paper snowflakes.

'This one here,' she says, pointing to a small bungalow on the front of the road. The skin on her pointing hand is pulled taut and shiny. I draw up carefully to the kerb, crunching over a band of thicker snow, then tell her to stay where she is until I come round and open the door for her. I put out my hand and she takes it long enough for me to feel how small and cold hers is, then lift one of the shopping bags from her and help her down. She says thanks and after searching in one of the bags hands me a bar of chocolate, tells me to give it to my son. I try to politely decline but she insists and so I thank her and take it, then hold the front gate for her and watch her make her way carefully towards her front door, her feet stepping in the same prints she made when leaving. Turning, she asks me my name. Perhaps she'll look for it when the final credits roll. I tell her and ask for hers.

'Agnes.'

'Have a good Christmas, Agnes.'

'You too, and safe journey.'

I nod and, slipping the chocolate into my pocket, get back in the car. As I'm starting the engine I see her open the front door before she disappears into the sudden shadows pooling in the hallway.

Mile after mile. Making the journey that feels as important as anything I've ever done since Daniel and which I have started to believe might be able to somehow change things if I pull it off, even set things back in an older balance before the plates tilted and everything fell askew. A white glare dazzles off the snow and I look around the car for my sunglasses that aren't there. I squint a little, drop the sun visor then suddenly breathe out heavily as a muster of crows lifts into the air, a ragged flapping black against the white.

My father bought an old gatekeeper's lodge at one of the entrances to the Sexton estate when it was being broken up. Small, but he says one of the internal walls can be knocked down and the whole place modernised for a quick turnaround. No one has lived in it for ten years and the windows are webbed and fly-trapped. He sends me into the roof space to check the state of the water tank. Almost the moment I push open the trapdoor and clamber in they are a moving black clot about my head, skittering shapes in the gloom pulsing about me, and I can't help myself screaming like some child, so it's a miracle that in my panic I don't plunge my foot through the ceiling plaster as I swing my torch and clutch at a rafter to try and hold my balance. Even now after all these years the thought of the bats makes my skin crawl. My father curses loudly when I tell him, the words spat out like he's hammering nails, and then swears me to silence. No one is to be told they were there, not a living soul, and when I don't understand he tells me that they are an endangered species and any disturbance of them could result in a fine. I'm shocked by my father's anger and confused by how anyone can value such creatures. He tells me that he needs to turn the place round as quickly as he can to recoup the outlay before the interest on the loan from the bank eats up all the profits. He asks me if I understand and I answer yes. That night we come back and smoke them out, then block up their entry point. I see them now in these crows lifting from the field, funnelling out from the roof, inky smudges staining the night sky.

I lower the window and try to spit the bad taste out of my mouth. And the legacy of my father lingers in at least one other thing and steps outside the realm of memory. Each night like he would do I check the plugs are out, do a tour of the house and assure myself that we are protected from whatever lurks in the night. But after I listen to my daughter breathing I return to the front door and, even though I've already done it, check that the chain lock is not in place, so that it can be opened with the key. No one is locked out. Our door isn't barred to our absent son. And each morning Lorna asks me with sleep still in her eyes if there's been any sign of Daniel. I tell her no without having to go to his room because I sleep lightly, drifting out of shallow dreams and instantly alert to the slightest sound, registering everything and trying to arrange it into a coherent pattern that will make sense of it all and guide me through to the dawn. A plane flying overhead, the ping of a moth against the bedroom window, a little rush of water running inexplicably along a pipe, the squeak of Lilly's headboard and light clink against our wall as she changes position – all these things must have their connection, be part of something greater, and if I can find the key that unlocks their meaning then I will perhaps slip into a restful sleep until the first light of morning. *Keep left. Drive for seven point three miles.* Sometimes at night she'll put a hot-water bottle in his bed – 'to take the chill off it,' she'll say. I suddenly realise that 'Snow in San Anselmo' has been on repeat for a long time. I couldn't get tickets for his seventieth birthday concert in East Belfast but later I watched the recording of it.

When it came to the end I cried without knowing why and was glad I was watching it on my own. In such moments I feel the flaring spark of a need to do more than I am called on by the daily requirements of my job. To make something that has value. To try and be more than myself.

I had an exhibition once in our local library but it wasn't a great success if I think only in commercial terms. Hardly anything sold and then only to people who knew me and wanted to be supportive. Maybe it's just an excuse for failure but I think where I live most people want pictures of sunsets over Dunseverick Castle, the snowy peaks of the Mournes or right now the Dark Hedges, preferably also with sunset, rainbow or some similar piece of extra-visual drama. So what do I want to take photographs of? It's hard to put it into words but I suppose the moment that lies just below the surface of things, or a glimpse of the familiar from a different angle.

Maybe I don't even know. But thinking about it as I drive, and listening to REM in the somehow reassuring knowledge that I've never heard a single one of their songs and understood what it was about, I try to make my eye register the photograph I'd like to take. But the vista ahead is partly blocked by a van emblazoned with Dial a Dog Wash and Pamper your Pooch. And those words blend with songs about orange crush, pushing elephants up the stairs and losing your religion so it's a confused mismatch, a tumbling dice of inconsequence and uncertainties. I never had a religion to lose but sometimes in moments of weakness I envy those who can navigate the big moments of life that mostly involve loss of some sort by drawing on the comfort of faith. Then, in these circumstances, anything that serves to prop you up, even for a while, seems not such a bad thing but I know it's not for me, not for Lorna, and although I hope not for our children it's their call at the end of the day.

'Where is Heaven?' Luke asks.

'I don't know. Up in the sky probably,' I answer Luke, reluctant to tell a young child that life merely ends in oblivion.

'Does everyone go there?'

'Only people who've been good,' I say, deciding that at least I should take parental advantage of this unexpected line of questioning.

'Do you have to be good all the time? What if you were bad just once or bad a little bit?'

'I suppose it's averaged out.'

'So God keeps a score? Writes it in a book?'

'Possibly,' I say, then look for some distraction to the questions.

A gritter passes me and even though I'm expecting it I'm still startled by the sound of the spray peppering the side of the car. A father pulls two children behind him on a wooden sledge that makes my plastic purchase look pathetic. So how's my scorecard reading? Depends perhaps on who's keeping it and if it's been averaged out. I remind myself of the deficits, some of which are a matter of public record – not in any legal sense but because they're familiar to those who know me – not least an over-readiness to take the easy path, to avoid any course of action that might bring more risks than I can handle. But the one I don't want to face I leave unvisited, unwilling to turn that stone. I'm not good under stress, not good at coping. I like everything composed and ordered inside the frame through which I view life and when things slip outside it I don't always deal well with it. I never want to think of the score Daniel would give me but because despite my best efforts the idea has lodged in my head I try to balance it with what might be thought of as my goodness, but there's nothing that can feel more unconvincing than trying to list your virtues to yourself.

They fragment and disappear into nothingness in an almost perfect synchronicity with the spray of water running off the windscreen. And I'm almost grateful when her voice interrupts, telling me to do this and do that, to follow this road and take that exit. Take the road to Luke and I can't think of him without thinking of that house in which he waits for me.

When we first saw them the rooms in the halls of residence shared a spartan neatness that at least had an interconnectedness and some vague sense of supervision, of someone watching over, if only to preserve their property, but in my memory where he is now has only an overwhelming sense of cavernous, hulking emptiness. An invisible land-lord and the old house which once probably laid claim to a certain grandeur dissected and partitioned, then filled with shabby furniture and basic equipment, its fabric and patina smudged and stained by too many hands and too much neglect. His room is at the very top under the roof which initially pleased him because it was bigger than his first-year room and because of its location seemed to offer the welcome possibility of privacy and a respite from the incessant noise and stir of a student house. I want to ring him but am frightened that he'll be sleeping and not pleased that I've woken him. For some reason there's a photograph that lingers in my memory and sharpens into focus when I think of Luke's house and it's one of Denis Thorpe's who took gritty black and white photographs of the north of England and worked for the *Guardian*. *Mr Lowry's Hat and Coat* – taken the day after the painter's death – shows two coats and hats hanging on pegs in a shadowed hallway, vaguely floral wallpaper, a dado rail. On one of the coats the lining is facing outward and catching something of the light. The photograph's about absence, an opened space and a stillness flowing into it, homing in on the relics of someone who once was but is no more.

Sometimes when I go into my children's rooms I have a strong sense of how closely our lives and the places we live bear each other's print. So it's as if their breathing is still present even in the empty room and all their memories and dreams are somehow seamlessly fused with the folds of a fabric or the grain of a surface. Only the coldness of technology remains impervious and no matter how often you let your fingers brush the keyboard of a computer, or the cover of a tablet, there is no sense of your absent child.

There's a password, a firewall that excludes you from finding any trace of its user's life so they stand separate from the rest of the room that everywhere else is infused with the full force of the being who claims this space. And that's why I think of Luke's house so much because if we press the print of ourselves into these spaces then it's also probable that they assert their realities in return, so that rabbit warren of empty rooms full of unmade beds and the scattered debris of hasty departures, the dark hallways and landings – all these things might force their collective presence into his senses. And right now when he's not well and the city he's staying in is weighted with snow it might lead him to view his life in a way that's not good for him so I want him to be home with his mother and father, in a house decorated and garlanded for Christmas no matter how much of that show is grounded in pretence.

As I head towards Gretna Green it's clear that the snow has been heavier and more recent, with thick slews at the side of the road, furrowed wheel tracks on the grey-slushed surface, and I pass a second-hand car dealer's where all the cars are white-humped and indistinguishable. For some reason images of holidays free-flow through the music and the satnav voice. Camping in Tollymore Forest – the night the tent nearly blew away – rented cottages in Cornwall and the phase of bodyboards and wetsuits, fossil hunting on Lyme Regis beach. Donegal in the rain and once, just once, in a heat wave. The unbearable heat of Turkey, so hot I wanted to spend much of the day in a dark room with a cold beer. The globe is grown smaller now, constricted through terror and yet the randomness of it might strike even where we feel most safe. The world has turned ever crazier since that day the planes flew into the towers and even before, so it makes me think that all you can do is hunker down with your family, find shelter in closeness, be permanently on what they call high alert, and hope the storm passes over your head. Even now as I drive I see small bouquets of artificial flowers tied to roadside poles and there must be others buried in the snow, waiting for the thaw of some spring to blossom once more into lurid colour. But these single offerings to single tragedies blur into swathes left after atrocities, a crush of layered flowers and tea lights flickering in the wind.

They pour scorn on the parents of those teenagers who run off to join Isis, claiming that they were either bad parents or must have known what was in their children's minds. At best their radar is faulty and so unaware of what was making its way into their homes to infect the minds of their children. Maybe once I would have felt the same. Just maybe. But that was before. Now I make no judgements or easy assumptions. And bringing up a child isn't like driving this car where I have the voice to guide me and, despite the snow, the tracks of other cars to follow, signals to tell me when to stop and when to go, warnings about possible hazards. Instead what you have is a kind of blizzard of conflicting and confusing ideas where, despite thinking you know the best direction to take, it soon becomes obvious that you've lost your way and the familiar landmarks that you put so much store by have disappeared in a white-out. There is the sound of a siren and for a second it makes me think I'm stumbling into the kind of danger that my imagination has been focused on and when I look in my mirror I see an ambulance with its blue lights flashing coming up quickly behind and I slow carefully then pull over to the side of the road, the car's tyres crunching on the frozen nuggets of grey ice that litter the debris field scattered by the snowploughs.

Luke has grown quiet, even quieter than before, and I worry about that. So I'd give just about anything if he would come to me with a question, even one I couldn't answer. But I know too that we've all grown quieter, with some part of ourselves needing to find shelter. Only Lorna refuses to follow that path and has become the cheerleader for the family, the one insisting on everything going on, maintaining the customs and rituals that every family has with a strength she draws from somewhere closed to me. I've always thought she was the stronger and she's proved it again and again, doing much of the heavy lifting, keeping us moving forward, ensuring that the outside tree has its decoration of lights. That's one of the many reasons I love her.

But I can't think of that love without being frightened because there are things I haven't told her and which I think I can't without risking everything I want and need. And sometimes I hear Daniel's voice and it's always in a whisper and without the cheery bantering tone that he likes to adopt so I know he's serious and he's threatening to tell her. I say that I'm going to tell her myself, tell her very soon – maybe when we get Christmas over – so he's wasting his time because unlike him I know how to offer the truth. But he doesn't believe me now any more than he believed the things I tried to make him understand. The flashing lights disappear into the distance. Someone else's pain, someone else's loss. I'm sorry for them but they're welcome to it and I can't share it because I've got

my own share and even a little more might be more than
I know how to bear.

The urgent voice on the phone wanted me at the hospital
and he needs me as soon as I can get there. It's the mater-
nity department at Dundonald where Lorna had ours.

Mother and newborn, but he doesn't tell me until
outside the side room that it's mother and stillborn. This
shouldn't be for me to see because it's a private moment
but he insists it's what she wants and suddenly I'm there
with a camera and she's sitting up tenderly cradling the
little girl and it's too late to walk away, much too late, so
I ask them if they're sure and they're both saying yes and a
phone photograph won't be good enough. I tell them she's
beautiful because I don't know what else to say and then
I take the photographs and worry that they'll be blurred
because my hands are shaking. Afterwards I print them up
and frame them as best I know how and I don't charge.

I think too of another photograph locked and hidden in
my camera that I've never shown Lorna and I feel sick until
I open the window and let the cold air rush about me.

A kestrel hovers in a field with its wings thrumming
the air. Further on there are two men wearing green
army-style clothing and carrying shotguns and I think
of Bruegel's *The Return of the Hunters*. The snow encom-
passes everything and as I pass Gretna I know it must
hide what little is left of the giant munitions factory
they built here during the Second World War and which
is now largely forgotten in our memory of those years.
But I remember the photographs I've seen somewhere
of the women who worked in the factory. A dangerous

job, often mixing volatile substances that got named the Devil's Porridge to make the propellant for shells. Not allowed to wear rings or earrings in case they caused a spark and set off an explosion. Called the Canary Girls because if they came into contact with sulphur it would turn their skin yellow. There is one particular photograph that I recall – it's a shot of a group of women taken at a distance so their dark figures look thin and spectral. They're preparing nitre that sits like a white mountain of salt. There's something ghostly about it, as if they're labouring in the underworld, and it contrasts with the more common group photos where the women swarm together in a tight phalanx of smiles, ill-fitting overalls and turban-style hair coverings.

They say people still come to Gretna to get married, come from all over the world, presumably because they think it's romantic getting married in a blacksmith's where previous generations of runaways turned up to pledge their vows. But maybe a forge isn't such a bad place to promise to spend the rest of your life with someone. And the more I think about it the more I believe that two people surviving together is a matter of strength of purpose and character, so those who made their vows amongst the irons and anvils did so surrounded by truer symbols than most of the weddings I get to see where they seem steeped in some sugary concoction of candyfloss and tinsel and look as if they might combust at the first spark of reality. I've come to believe over the years that there's an inverse ratio between marital longevity and the lavishness of the wedding day. So if that theory is correct at least half of those I've photographed probably collapsed when the first cold wind blew. And there's no dignity any more for some people.

Even setting aside the orange spray tans that always require colour adjustment, they want to copy things they've seen on YouTube so they're doing a dance down the aisle or the groom and his groomsmen are performing some boy-band sequence. Themed weddings, wedding favours, doves, sky lanterns, ice sculptures – so much debris falling on my head like confetti, even though in most places they're not actually allowed to throw the stuff any more unless it's bio-degradable. So as I pass the town I feel some respect for it, as it was, if not now they've probably turned it into a theme park with a tourist shop and fifty-seven varieties of shortbread and kilted kitsch.

Biting the hand that feeds me, thinking like that. And I don't even have to stay to the death when the drink's in and if there's going to be mayhem it's the time to cry havoc. All those smouldering family tensions, all those drink-loosened inhibitions and flirtations set free like the sky lanterns. Ready to burn the house down.

Somehow Lorna and I have stayed together. And I'm grateful for that, frightened of doing anything that would put us in danger, so I have to think things out on this journey but I don't know if the monochrome world I'm travelling through makes it easier or harder. Things are more complicated than choosing between what I think is right and what I don't know is wrong. The snow conceals everything but I'm not sure if I can go on covering what for the moment is hidden and I'm not always a strong person inside so I'm frightened that like some sudden thaw I'll let it out when she's not expecting it and when it's not the right time to release it.

We never had a wedding album, nothing except a few photographs taken by my sister, and if we had, what would it have shown except things that we don't want reminding of? It wasn't a dream day where we were bathed in the well-wishes of family and friends. A registry-office job and a few sandwiches and drinks back at the flat we were already sharing. Hard to make an album out of that. But none of the paltriness of the day's ceremonies or the negatives of the events surrounding it can ever stop me thinking of it as the very best thing I've ever done and would do a thousand times over.

Lorna's going to help you, I get told when I enter the primary school on the first of two days during which I'm taking individual and class photographs. It's my first ever school job and I'm nervous. I've done a police clearance check, got the certificate to prove that I'm not a threat to children. And what I notice about her is that when she smiles everything else falls away and she steps out of what some might see as her unassuming self and becomes beautiful. She smiles a lot. At the children, at the teachers, even at me, and not when I try to say something funny but when I do something stupid like stumble over the lights. She seems to know so many of the children by name even though she's a classroom assistant with a particular set of responsibilities. And she's good at organising them, getting them into the right places, coaxing the unenthusiastic and calming the hyper. Without her I know the day would be a nightmare but she's got everything under control and the children respond to her in a way that seems relaxed but respectful. She hunkers down a lot when she's talking to the younger children and sometimes she touches their hair or lays her hand across their shoulders when they're animated, as if they were her own. I try to be as good as she is with them but I don't think I quite manage it. And to be honest it's a nightmare job because never working with children or animals applies to photographers as well as actors as they've an uneasy relationship with stillness and an unpredictable tendency to facial tics, blinking, grimacing, looking in the wrong place and generally pulling faces at the wrong moment. With one you can mostly manage it through bribery or distraction but when there's a group of them that's another challenge altogether. Getting everyone sitting straight and looking at the camera requires either luck or some kind of magic spell that momentarily freezes them. She could see that I was struggling and so she came and stood at my shoulder, got them all to focus on her just long enough for me to click.

She's always been able to see when I'm struggling, always come and stood at my side. Sees it without me having to say anything and there've been times when I've struggled a lot. There was the year when I got depressed, not the absolute black depths that some plunge into and are left unable to function but enough for me to glimpse the misery of the condition. I didn't even know I was at the start and soon the way you feel is just the way you feel and you begin to believe that it's normal, and to forget that there was a different time. It was her who made me go to the doctor's and get help. It's Lorna too who sees if there's a time when I momentarily dip and helps me through it.

What I needed on that day was a cup of tea and at break she invited me to the staffroom. Not the teachers' staffroom but a store under the stairs where classroom assistants, ancillary and office staff hung out. A few chairs, a table and a small kitchen area. About half a dozen women getting their break and sharing a laugh. The school cook in whites and apron, large, her face florid as if she'd just looked in a hot oven, hearing I was the photographer soon piped up, 'So, Tom, do you think we could do a *Calendar Girls* shoot?' Lots of giggling, Lorna embarrassed.

'I don't see why not, but what's your charity?' I asked, taking a cup of tea from Lorna. The builder's tea she still makes. 'And you need a theme.'

'Charity? More like our retirement fund. There's no sign of our lottery syndicate getting us out of here.'

'You only need to win once,' claims a woman in the corner without looking up from checking her phone, the tone suggesting she's offered a profundity.

'Well my suggested theme would be school, naturally, things from all our jobs. I have a couple of very large colanders out in the canteen I could put to use because as you can see, Tom, I'm a woman not unfamiliar with a fish supper.'

More giggles, the women enjoying my embarrassment. Me trying to smile and pretending to be studying my tea.

'And you know what I'm going to do if our numbers come up? I'm going to send the school-meals department in Academy Street a menu from some swanky hotel in the Caribbean and ask them what they think I should have for starters.'

Everyone laughing. Someone coming in from playground duty and flicking the kettle on the boil again. Lorna taking my cup to wash it and then showing me round the assembly hall again. A complete day of children: children with grazed knees, earrings and missing baby teeth, assorted twins, children of every ethnic background, children with extravagantly double-barrelled first names and some with an inexhaustible need to torment the person beside them.

63

And she's smiling all the way through it and every melt-down and tiny trauma and children who need to go to the toilet and some who don't want to be in a photograph because they've been in one before. So what I took from those first encounters was that she was someone with an infinite sense of patience and that's a virtue I'm grateful she possesses because I guess there's been times when she's needed it with me and the rest of us.

Driving this car ever closer to Luke I have entered a world that in part is beautiful but in its endless sweep remorse-less and cold, indifferent to all other life. I try to evoke Christmas to dispel the shiver of that feeling and am momentarily helped by passing a man wheeling a bicycle with a Christmas tree stretched from the saddle across the handlebars. The hacked base of the trunk suggests he's lib-erated it from some woodland rather than bought it. He's gone all too quickly and I'm left once more with the soft plumpness of white fields but the road ahead stretching into an increasingly glittering eye-dazzling sharpness.

She wore an engagement ring and I didn't think of her other than as someone who was good at being kind and the pres-sure of getting my business up and running was more than enough for me to concentrate on. I'd worked for a maga-zine for a couple of years and I'd reached the end of the line in shooting the Association of Chartered Accountants or golf-club dinners, the opening of some new boutique fashion shop or school reunions. The unsocial hours didn't help and to be always looking through the lens at someone else who was having a good time, or at least pretending to be, had reached a point where it was beginning to do my head in. And a couple of times I was careless in noting names so I married people off who were married to other people and there were a few indignant complaints, almost as if they'd been publicly outed as members of some swingers' club.

I hadn't seen Lorna for three months when I got a call from the school to take photographs of their sports day. All the traditional stuff – sack races, egg and spoon, three-legged – with the new ethos that discourages competition so prizes for everyone and the only hard edges came in the mothers' races where elbows were much in use. Not enough fathers had turned up to run one. There was something that seemed different about her and it wasn't just the new, shorter hairstyle. She was quieter, smiled a little less and was more at the edge of things than I recalled. Then towards the end she held her arms out wide to a child with special needs and that smile broke across her face and suddenly rendered her beautiful and I knew I felt something. That's why, without embarrassing us both, I managed discreetly to include her in a photograph. And it was her photograph that I first fell in love with.

But I knew too that was something I used to do at regular intervals. At some function or other there would always be a woman in my photographs who I fastened on, secretly attributing a life to her, a personality, and in the absence of a real girlfriend would imagine that she returned my love. Said like that it sounds creepy but these were fleeting unsubstantiated feelings generated by loneliness and a desire to share my life with someone. I suppose if Facebook had existed then I would have continued my feelings for Lorna by looking for her online, learning what

I could about her, trying to cross her path with my own, but the most I did was drive past the school a couple of times when it wasn't the quickest route to where I was going. And there was the engagement ring on her finger to shadow whatever hopes I might have harboured.

A car pulling a grey caravan passes in the opposite direction, its roof striped with snow so it looks like a badger on wheels. My track record with women wasn't great. A couple of short-term fizzle-outs and one relationship that lasted just under a year before she decided it wasn't going anywhere and called it a day. I don't know even now where it was she wanted it to go and as for me I wanted it to lead to happiness and above all something secure. Something on which you could depend.

The phone rings and it startles me, pulling me too suddenly back to the moment.

'Hi, Dad, are you still in Scotland?' Lilly asks.

'I've just left Scotland and am heading towards a place called Carlisle.'

'There's a girl in my class whose second name is Carlisle.'

'Perhaps that's where she came from then? Does your mother know you're using her phone?'

'She says it's OK. Is there lots of snow?'

'Lots and lots. I've bought you a sledge. It's nothing fancy, made of plastic but should do the job. When I get back we can go sledging in Stormont if you like.'

'Can Luke come too?'

'If he's well enough he can come. Put your mum on.'

'What does Santa say when his wife asks him what the weather's like?'

'I don't know, what does Santa say when his wife asks him what the weather's like?'

'Reindeer.'

'Very good, Lilly, very good. Now put Mum on.'

She asks me how I'm doing, what the roads are like, am I going to make it and I tell her yes I'm going to make it, that barring something unseen we'll catch the last sailing if we miss the earlier one. As soon as I've said it I regret using the words 'something unforeseen' because right away it plants a seed of doubt in both our minds and we don't need to let that grow because if we give it free rein then we'll be able to imagine things that aren't going to be good for either of us. So as a distraction I ask her if she's switched the outside lights on yet but she tells me it's not dark enough and she'll do it later in the afternoon. Then she tells me I shouldn't be on the phone when I'm driving and we end the conversation.

I still keep that first photograph in my wallet. Cropped down to the size of a postage stamp so it's just her head and she's not looking at the camera, doesn't know that I've caught her smile. After all these years she's still never seen it and I keep it because I like how she is in that moment with her face turned in praise towards a child without pose or artifice and that makes it different to most of the photographs I spend my life taking. I'd like to be able to tell her the next time we speak that this is what I've always liked most about her.

And how I got to find her was through my short-lived attempt at photographing the natural world which was what brought me to the towpath that summer morning but with nothing to show for it except a heron on the far bank that looked like a metal garden statue and a

67

blurred out-of-focus image of what might or might not have been a kingfisher. A pathetic return but one at least that made me understand that I didn't have either the patience or knowledge to go down that road. Then just as I was deciding to pack it in there was a jogger coming along the path, head down with a fine sheen of sweat on her bare shoulders, and as I stepped back to let her pass she lifted her face to say thanks and in that second we recognised each other. I thought she was going to run on but she stopped, dropped her hands to her hips and said, 'Hi.' Her voice was breathless and I think she was embarrassed and as a distraction asked me what I was doing. In that moment I would have swopped lions in the Serengeti, killer whales, dolphins dancing, just for the chance to take one photograph of her as I tried not to stare while explaining about attempting to capture the wildlife of the river.

Then we ran out of things to say until I heard myself asking did she want to get a coffee or a cold drink and didn't quite believe that it was actually me who had spoken the words and for a second wondered if some invisible ventriloquist had said them on my behalf. Her glance at her watch made me think that she was going to say no and I was already trying to compose some face-saving get-out for both of us when she said yes and smiled, not one of those transforming smiles but the neutral type you might give when a stranger opens a door for you. So we sit outside at the Lock Keeper's Inn and she has bottled water as we try to think of things to say. There's no engagement ring. Maybe she doesn't wear it when she runs. Something to ponder but then things just become easy and whatever nervousness I'm feeling fades and we talk, talk through two coffees and two slices of lemon drizzle cake. Afterwards we walk back to the car park and my heart is doing whatever hearts are supposed to do in situations like this but which always sounds stupid whatever word you choose to describe it because I know when we reach the cars I'm going to work up the courage to ask for her phone number. And courage isn't something I've ever felt I possess in any great measure.

The images of a stone-still heron, a blurred flash of colour that might have been a kingfisher and a phone number – best morning's work I've ever done. You can torment yourself by thinking too much about the role of fate or even simple coincidence in affecting the course of your life and I think there's nothing much to be gained from it except some vicarious thrill of ships in the night and roads not taken. Sometimes now as I drive through the snow I see individuals out walking but there's no obvious source of their journey or destination. So what is the purpose of this dark-coated figure's slow walk past the metal railings of an industrial estate or this young woman's trudge along a road that appears to connect neither homes nor shops? It feels like these journeys speak silently of an unsolved mystery at the heart of our daily lives and once I see a young man who looks like Daniel and as I pass him I turn my head to try and see his face but it is hidden under his hooded cowl. As I leave him behind I catch him in my side mirror and see my son raise his hand and slowly lower his hood, then he isn't there any more and there are no footprints in the snow.

Keep left. Drive for eight point seven miles. Listen to the music. Let the rhythm and the words fill the opening space. Robert

Wyatt with his wonderfully wonky English voice that I like and I try to follow him into the songs and think of building ships when we could be diving for pearls but there are other insistent voices that refuse to be pushed aside so easily. And if everything with Lorna had been straightforward then I tell myself that perhaps nothing would have formed strong enough to endure but if I am given a choice I would want to try and arrive at where we are through a different path. So it was a naïve foolishness to think that the exchange of phone numbers secured or sealed anything and, if it paved the way, the year that was to come filters through my senses and nothing can be dulled or set to the side. It feeds its pulse into the series of lights in the car's dashboard, in the brake lights of the van in front, the very rhythm of the music, and makes me want to tell the woman in the satnav who's talking to me now in her pitch-perfect voice that she's no idea what it was like.

So there asserting his right to his place in the story is Johnston Bailey, the man who gave her the ring and someone who if he was to step out in front of my car right now would see me press the accelerator rather than the brakes. So he thinks the ring signifies ownership and isn't prepared to relinquish what he sees as his entitlement and all that time I'm so bewildered how someone like Lorna could link herself with a piece of shit like him that it makes me think her relationship with me might be hopelessly misjudged if in a different way. He's from the same area of the city and they went to the same school together so right from the start I feel the insecurity of what they have shared and I shall always be an outsider to that. He works as some kind of partner in a company that hires out skips and I find out enough about him to believe that he has at the very least a peripheral connection to an organisation that claims to defend its community but makes its lucrative living off it through the full range of extortion and drug dealing. I don't think that he's directly involved but it's soon obvious that he knows people who are. And at first, if I'm honest, I felt she was tarnished by her relationship with this man and I couldn't understand how it had happened but soon what I felt for her was stronger than anything else and I know now I'd no right to my silent judgement.

We go out and I never ask her about him and what happened between them, waiting until she's ready to tell me and there's also a part of me that doesn't wish to know, just wants to live in the present with the happiness I'm feeling but still too frightened to put all my faith in. But soon I realise there's something wrong and maybe it's because I spend so much of my time looking at faces that I've become sensitive to changes and understanding what states of mind they might signify.

Eventually she tells me as much as she's willing to, so he's still calling her up all the time, sometimes late at night when he's had a few drinks, and he's talking about them getting back together, that they were 'right for each other' and it was only a matter of time before she realised it. Then he hears about me and things turn bad. So she's supposed to owe him the money for things he's bought her and the holiday he took her on and when the calls become abusive and threatening she blocks him on her phone. When she talks of going to the police her family argue against it and tell her she'd put them all at risk because in some people's eyes there's no bigger crime than 'touting'. The best they can offer is that they'll try to talk to someone who might be able to have a word, warn him off, but it seems they don't know anyone high enough up the food chain. Her parents and brothers look at me with barely concealed resentment as if I'm the cuckoo in the nest and a poor substitute for Lorna's previous.

One night after I've left her off I drive to the end of her street, a street that has a paramilitary mural on the final gable wall with three black-clad figures in balaclavas holding guns. The figures however are amateurishly painted which serves to weaken the intended image of menace. I am about to turn on to the main road when there's three guys suddenly standing in front of the car and before I have a chance to react one of them has opened my door and I find myself looking at Bailey for the first time. He has to bend down to speak to me so our faces are closer than I want them to be and he asks me my name even though he knows who I am. I'm not taking my eyes off him but trying also to be aware of where the other two are.

'I know who you are,' he says when I don't answer him. 'And I thought it was time you and me had a talk. So why don't you get out of the car.'

He's wearing a short-sleeved T-shirt and it looks like he works out but his face is thin and almost sharpened into the point of his chin and it makes him seem as if he's borrowed someone else's body. I try to appear casual, disguise the fear I'm feeling.

'What is it you want to say?' I ask without showing any inclination to get out.

'You're somewhere people don't like strangers. You're somewhere you don't belong.' When I still don't say anything, he offers, 'And there's no guaranteeing your safety. Do you understand what I'm saying?' He looks over my shoulder and sees a camera on the back seat. 'Do you work for a newspaper?' Then when I tell him no he says he'll give me some advice which turns out to be that I should fuck off and not show my face again around Lorna if I know what's in my best interests. That my type aren't wanted and I should do myself a favour by walking away and not looking back. When he stands back up straight I shut the door and press the button that locks all the doors. As I start to drive away all three blatter at the car with their feet.

Until that moment I'd got through my life without ever having a fight, without ever being threatened, and if I'm honest I'm probably someone no one really notices very much and the only time they do is when I've a camera in my hand and I'm asking them to, so I was pretty shook up and unsure about what I would do. I'd already understood that involving the police was considered an unacceptable and dangerous form of behaviour and that, in this world I'd stumbled into, normal rules didn't apply. So as I drove and tried to work out my response I consoled myself with fantasies that involved retaliatory acts of violence with purchased guns or the hiring of a hit man, played out stupid improbable scenarios in my head and tried to use them to stem the spreading flare of humiliation, fear, and then in their wake the rising wave of anger. And did I ever think of taking the advice and walking away? I don't think I did, I don't think that I ever did, and I'm glad because this allows me to stem some of the curse of this memory and leaves me in a place which although precarious is where just for a moment I can feel better about myself. I had to decide whether to tell Lorna or keep it from her but in my life I've come to understand that lies mostly lead to disaster – that's why in soaps everyone lies to each other all the time, and it's these same lies that eventually and inevitably end in some form of car crash. A car crash that might make compulsive viewing but isn't something you ever want to experience in the flesh. When I told her she too was angry and then apologetic as if ashamed of what had happened and almost suggesting that it was her fault.

Past a white-roofed church where either someone has got lucky in their timing or had a spiritual and meteorological insight into the coming weather, with the large poster on the noticeboard near the entrance proclaiming, 'Though your sins be as scarlet they shall be white as snow.' And I think it's true even now that although we never talk about this time we both feel as if in part our early days together bore the stain of something that had fastened on to us and which we didn't know how to shake off.

'Perhaps we should cool it, take a break and see how things work out,' she says as we sit in my car looking out over the sea.

'Is that what you want?' I ask, frightened of the answer.

'No, it's not what I want.'

I reach across and take her hand, all my relief transmitted into a simple tightening of my grip.

'I'm frightened,' she says. 'He's unpredictable and now he's behaving like this I don't know what he might do. And he knows people.'

The sea is wind-worried, the waves white-tipped and churlish, but there is an underlying steadiness as if nothing's happening that's not meant to. There is an island whose name I don't know.

'Maybe that's where we should go and live,' I tell her, pointing towards it and not telling her that I'm frightened too.

'I think you can walk out to it when the tide's out. Need to watch you don't get cut off.'

Living on an island, cut off from everything that wishes you harm – that's what seems the very best of things.

'What are we going to do?' I ask her, because even then I needed her to be the one telling me what was best.

She says she doesn't know and we both sit and stare silently at the sea for a while. Looking back it's always tempting to reshape things so that you come out better but it would be a lie if I try to pretend that in those days I was anything other than lacking in direction and blind-sided by every fear let loose in my head. And although I don't know if I did so then, now when I think of those days they always merge in jagged edges with that night when my father smoked the bats out of their nesting place and I watched the tight black funnel emerging from the roof and then splintering into skittering single shapes.

The sea seems to fall momentarily into a greater sense of calm. There is a bobbing black head of a seal which disappears almost as soon as we have identified what it is.

'You're not to come to the house any more. We'll meet in the town and I'll get a taxi home. And I'm going to move out and get a place of my own when I've saved up a bit.'

'Maybe things will blow over,' I say. 'Maybe he'll wise up. See he's wasting his time.'

But she doesn't seem convinced by my attempt at optimism and into the silence that follows flow all the doubts and imaginings that deep anxiety has the power to generate. I try to find a pleasure in her presence that might dispel them, look at her hair, the side of her face as she stares at the sea, but wonder if I'll be able to see her fully smile again. I want to hold her close but when I eventually do I know that I'm holding all those worries tight and nothing seems able to ease the stiffness out of her body.

Soon after, I turn up at my studio to find someone has spray-painted the word *Paedo* in large letters across the shutter on the front door that I can't fully remove despite scrubbing at it while enduring the accusatory stare of every passer-by. I come to think that there is the real possibility of having petrol poured through a broken window and the place set on fire. But I can't afford the cost of security cameras and so each morning's journey to the studio is fraught with fear about arriving at a pile of smouldering ash. And I tell the woman speaking to me through the satnav whose perfectly modulated voice is calm that living with fear is the worst way to live and that it darkens even the bright things you try to do and that it's incessant, gnawing away at the very things you need to exist. So there comes a point when your anger about what's happening to you boils up, overflows, and you become willing to consider any remedy, however desperate or foolhardy it might seem to the rational mind you once possessed.

After the spray-paint job and then subsequent damage to my car and finally a bullet in an envelope, I enter what I guess is a fight-or-flight moment and I can't flee without losing Lorna so I find myself sitting outside his business yard, watching the comings and goings, following his car at lunchtime to the cafe, the bookie's or the football supporters' club he seems to frequent. I start with stupid childish things like ordering skips from payphones to be delivered to different addresses across the city, tell myself he'll think he's in a turf war with another firm, be distracted. Then I discover when you take a step forward, even a small step, the fear doesn't exercise such a tight grip. It's still there but it's somehow reduced and you allow yourself to feel less of a helpless victim because ultimately it's the sense of powerlessness that does you in.

And with each small step you gain the desire to go bolder because wounding isn't ever going to be enough – there has to be a final fatal blow. But I can't think of how this might be achieved without going close up and I don't yet have the courage for this.

With our troubled legacy of history I guess there's a network out there of self-employed shooters and enforcers whose services are employed in drug wars, internecine factional disputes over territory and simple old-fashioned score settling. But they don't advertise themselves in the papers or online and I don't know the type of people who know this type of people.

The slow ferment of hatred. Schemes and dreams. The business operates out of a Portakabin in the corner of the yard. They only have one vehicle to deliver the skips. It's flaking with rust in parts and looks like it should be consigned to one of the skips it carries. This business isn't raking in profits. The signs warning of security cameras and a security firm with guard dogs have been bought off the Internet and I don't imagine there's much worth stealing in the dilapidated building that acts as an office. The windows are protected by wire grilles and the night I climb over the wall and take a close look round there is enough light for me to see that damp has seeped into the side walls leaving them with a bulging blister and weeds grow out of the guttering. A row of yellow skips lines the back wall of the yard. One of them is loaded to the brim with what looks like household junk, as if some house has been turned upside down and all its contents shaken out. I start to think that this would be the perfect place for a body. Wrapped in an old carpet, covered with a layer of debris to be buried in some landfill site. Buried and forgotten. This of course is all fantasy. And what happens is a crime of a different nature.

Without telling me until afterwards Lorna goes to see him and she's vague about what happened, what she said, and even now all these years later she doesn't want to talk about it and I know not to push her. But I can't ever get it out of my head that it should have been me dealing with him and if that's just a bit of hurt masculine pride it still smarts. But I'm also filled with admiration for someone who had the courage to face him. And perhaps his hurt pride is mollified by the arrival of a new love in his life. Much younger and almost instantly carrying his child and he has other things to give his attention to as well as this newly acquired family because he's involved in some drugs-deal fallout and soon decamps to Spain where he sinks his money into a share of a bar. The word is that it's not safe for him to return and we outwardly forget about him but when ten years later his death is reported in the press – a stabbing in front of his bar after a late-night dispute with some locals over an unpaid debt – my quiet relief is challenged by Lorna's sense of shock and upset that at first I find bewildering and then come to accept as part of the complexity of life. I say something wrong and she's angry with me for days so it almost feels as if his shadow is still lingering over us but eventually I understand that being married to someone and however close you are doesn't entitle you to own their memories or be part of their story before you met.

For a while I've been making good time but when I pass Carlisle and start heading eastwards the conditions worsen. From my previous journeys I remember that everywhere on this part seems to start with an H – Haltwhistle, Hayden Bridge, Hexham – and I encounter roads less well-cleared and where there is something in the sky that seems to suggest that the snow hasn't finished with them. *At the fourth roundabout take the first exit on to the A69.* There are fewer signs of life getting back to normal and everywhere feels as if they're bunkered down for a longer haul.

Perhaps it's to do with the closeness to the Pennines and I'm grateful that I don't have to venture further south towards them because in my imagination they have taken on the feel of something akin to the Himalayas. And I never think of snow and mountains without seeing that photograph of George Mallory and his wife with their eyes wide and slightly startled as if something unexpected has crossed their vision, and the side of her hair is a darker shadow separating their faces, making it easy to think of it as a portent, and there are times when I've looked at someone my camera is focused on and I believe in that moment, just as it did for them, the subject's future life has flickered across their consciousness. He carried a photograph of her in the pocket of his tweed jacket to leave on the summit and when they found that desiccated body with the frozen skin bleached white like alabaster there was no trace of it. So I like to think that just maybe against all the odds he did reach Everest's summit and that disaster happened on his descent, but even though I don't want to, sometimes, despite my best efforts, I think too of that fall – the sudden spinning into darkness away from the solidity of rock and into the nothingness of frozen air. Did he see her face in those final moments or was everything just a plunging fear-blinded loss of consciousness and loss of self? I guess it's no longer possible that they'll find that image but I believe it's still there, formed out of particles of memory and love, existing in some place where time can't ever annihilate it.

Keep on the A69. The voice pulls me back to the moment. I'm hungry now but not willing yet to give up travel time to eat more of the provisions Lorna has organised and because I moved the coolbox behind the passenger seat I can't reach it. So I try just to keep on going but hunger is like an itch and as soon as you're aware it's there it nags away until you are compelled to respond but there isn't an immediate or obvious place to stop safely. She tells me again to *Stay on the A69* where I start to pass signs for Hadrian's Wall. All through history young men, and now sometimes women, huddling against the cold or the heat, wondering what their purpose is and dreaming of home. Belfast, Helmand, Hadrian's Wall. They say the length of the wall is a popular walk for hikers now and in Belfast we've made the most of our past troubles and package them for tourists in soft-focused bus and taxi tours of murals and the peace wall. Decades after the Germans got rid of the Berlin Wall we've still got ours and I'm never sure why we call it the peace wall when its original purpose was to prevent the ease with which communities living in close proximity might attack each other. Now such interactions are generally limited to the occasional lobbing of missiles – golf balls seem especially popular but I don't imagine many of those doing so play that particular sport, so I don't know where they get them.

I don't know either what purpose our troubled days had and I'm grateful that I wasn't the guy arriving with a camera at each scene of atrocity, trying to measure up the public effectiveness of an image against respect for the privacy of individual suffering. But as a languid drift of snow starts to fall I am mindful of the right image's power to impact on our consciousness. So I think of the little boy lying in the surf on a Turkish beach, drowned trying to reach a Greek island in a plastic dinghy.

And even though I forget his name I do remember the feeling that it produced and I know that somehow for a time, however short it proved, it changed things. Changed more than any reporter's words or politician could do because in a photograph there's nothing between you and the subject, nothing to sanitise or mitigate – it's just you there in that moment as close as the camera places you and held still and silent.

Sometimes it's closer than we want to be, so there is no escape from those Vietnamese children running towards us with their bodies burned by napalm or the bewildered stare of the Syrian boy sitting traumatised in the back of an ambulance, and perhaps because it's more recent I remember his name was Omran.

I pull into the cleared entrance to a farm shop. One side of the door has a row of Christmas trees huddling white-branched against each other and the other holly wreaths bedecked with baubles and red ribbons. There is a large homemade sign declaring 'Business as Usual' hung above the entrance and someone has drawn holly leaves in felt tip round the lettering. The memory of the children in the photographs and the falling snow has made me desperate to talk to Luke, both to reassure myself he's still OK and to try to invest all my hope in a safe future untouched by trauma or one of those random and fatal encounters with the deranged or purely evil – a madman looking for a fight – that litter the news headlines and make every parent stop in their tracks then seek to find comfort in the ineffectual reassurance that statistically it's not likely to be your child. But after what has happened I know that this is meaningless and I think of the woman in the school store under the stairs telling us that you only have to win once and how easily this might become the only one time you lose. He takes just long enough to answer his phone to allow me to torture myself with a flail of dark imaginings so when I speak my first words they contain both a mixture of irritation and relief.

'Are you all right, Luke?' I ask, unable to stop the urgency pressing into my voice.

'I'm OK. Where are you now? Is there something wrong?'

It's not impatience I hear but something closer to longing and so I reassure him that I'm not so far away, about an hour and a half all being well.

'What are the roads like?' he asks, as he did the last time I spoke to him.

'Not so bad but it's starting to snow again. Nothing heavy, though.'

'It's not snowing here,' he says and I know he must be on or in his bed looking up at the skylight.

'Are you keeping warm? Is there any heating on in the house?'

'The landlord has it on some kind of timer – early in the morning and then at night so there's not a lot about. But I'm staying in bed so it's not so bad.'

'Your mother's lit a fire at home.'

'I thought we weren't allowed to.'

'She thinks Christmas makes it a special circumstance. Her and Lilly are toasting marshmallows.'

'Don't think that'll help Santa.'

'Luke, do you know why Santa always comes down the chimney?'

'No, why does he?'

'Because it suits him.'

'Did Lilly tell you that?'

'Yes, and listen, when we get you home and you're feeling well again she'd like to go sledging with you. All of us. We can go into the grounds of Stormont. What do you say?' And it feels as if I'm asking him one of the most important questions I've ever done.

'Sure, if the snow hasn't melted by then, and I've got a bit of work to do over the holidays. I've to make a five-minute film on a particular location and add music.'

'Got anywhere in mind?'

'Yes, I want to film it in Roselawn.'

'Roselawn – the cemetery?' I ask, unsure if I've heard him right, and there are so many things springing to my lips that I struggle to stifle them.

'I don't mean to shock you or anything but yes that's where. There's a part of it I saw and it's a separate sec- tion from all the rows of headstones. It's not like anything I've ever seen. I went back on my own and took some photographs. I'll send them to you if you want to see them. It's a part of the cemetery where people have personalised the burial place of whoever – it's really weird, with plastic flowers, football scarves and figures, all sorts of ornaments and decorations on the branches of trees. And there's lots of wind chimes so I thought I would incorporate them into the music.'

'Do you not think it's a bit morbid?'

'It's not a place that feels like it's to do with death so much as the lives that people once had. It feels like it's full of their memories. But I'm not asking you to take me.'

'I'll take you.'

'Are you sure? I'll understand if you don't want to.'

'I'll take you,' I tell him with no pretence of enthusiasm. 'We don't need to let your mother know.'

He agrees and then he's gone. So the call I had hoped would lead to a sense of reassurance about the future only amasses new anxieties. It's not a place I want to go back to and I'm surprised my son thinks it's somewhere he should film. But I'll go there and watch over him. My father's there too. A father who never saw my wife or my children. His hands shaking so much towards the end that I wanted to clasp him tightly just to make it stop. And it feels as if everything is shaking now with this fine fret of snow slanting slowly down, the wind casually brushing the branches of some of their burden, the collective tremble of the whitened world I'm driving into. *Keep straight on*. Straight on and steady – it's what I must do now, despite everything. Just concentrate on the road that's visible, not look too far ahead or let my eyes be dazzled by the light that radiates from all around me. At my father's funeral when I was going out to the street to lead the mourners my mother called me back – it was the tradition that only men followed the coffin – and handed me the two envelopes that I'd left behind. 'For the gravediggers,' she whispered and I put them inside the jacket pocket of the suit I had bought the day before and had almost forgotten to pull one of the labels off. My mother's small-town community believed that in all things and not least in death there were rituals and proprieties that should be observed. I was impatient of them but have come to understand their importance, if not to the dead then to the living.

It's always cold in Roselawn, wintry and exposed to rain and wind, but perhaps it's because that's often the time when old people die. The minister labours on and I grow impatient as I search for whatever it is I'm supposed to be feeling and then with the last Amen I hand the envelopes to the gravediggers who stand a little way off and lean on their long-handled shovels and they touch their foreheads in a gesture that feels like it comes from a different century. Now of course there is another reason I don't want to go back there but if it's what Luke feels he wants to do I know I have to help him even if it's only to drive him there and back, sit in the car and wait.

You spend a lot of time driving and waiting on your children, hours and hours and sometimes the waiting turns into slow time. Luke had a girlfriend for six months during his last year at school but allowing them to get together involved me driving him into Belfast, dropping him off and then picking him up again later at night.

Staying dry between the drives, not allowed to arrive a moment earlier than the designated time, not knocking on the door of her house but announcing my arrival by sending a text and then waiting until he deigned to appear. I always used to write, 'Taxi here,' but even though I thought those journeys home might have been an opportunity to talk it never worked out like that and they passed mostly in silence because it seemed whatever was in his mind, or was important to him, was left behind and conversation was just a distraction. Some nights I thought that if I had been a taxi driver he might have felt more obligation to talk.

Once, after thinking about it on the drive to get him from Amber's, I decided it was right to tell him something about myself that he didn't know and that in the sharing of it something personal would be brought into existence between us.

'Luke, there's something I want to tell you, could you come off your phone for a second.'

He knows that requests to disengage from phones are always a prelude to something of possible significance and although we've banned them from our evening-meal table we don't ask very often because I know it's the teenage equivalent of leaving the mother ship and floating away untethered into the emptiness of space. He stops scrolling and holds it in his right hand. Sometimes when it's as close as this I've felt the urge to reach across, grasp it, then dispatch it through my side window.

But I remain steady and only glance at him. I can tell he's started to feel appropriately nervous.

'Is there something wrong between you and Mum?' he asks.

'No there's not. Why did you say that?'

'Amber's parents are splitting up.'

'Sorry to hear that. Is she upset?'

'Says she's not bothered, that they're always arguing anyway. So maybe it's for the best.'

'Who will she live with?'

'I don't know – her mother probably. Did you and Mum ever think of splitting up?'

'You never listen to Al Green but if you did you'd know one of your mum's favourite songs of his is "Let's Stay Together".'

'I don't think favourite songs stop people splitting. What is it you want to tell me?'

I'm backtracking from the idea but can't think of a convincing substitute and seeing he's in a 'just say what you need to say so that I can get back to my phone' frame of mind, I tell him without soft-soaping or hesitation.

'A while back I was depressed. I didn't know at first that I was, just couldn't get my head up and didn't feel right. Your mother made me go to the doctor's and he told me I was depressed. I wasn't the worst type or anything – just not feeling like I was supposed to. Anyway, she put me on some low-dose pills and after a while things got better.'

He doesn't say anything but I think he's listening. How I've said it doesn't do any justice to what happened or what I want to tell him. His phone beeps and to his credit he only glances downwards for a second.

'And the reason I'm telling you this is because if you ever find that things aren't right in your head you need to talk to someone and not bottle it up. You understand what I'm saying?'

He nods and when silence ensues and it's clear that I've nothing more to say he looks at his phone and then begins to text. Amber's parents decide not to split and the only break-up comes a month later when she texts to say that she doesn't want to go out with him any more. And if songs don't stop people splitting, when it does happen sometimes they help by offering whatever it is you want to say and so for a couple of nights I hear him listening on repeat to 'Last Night I Dreamt That Somebody Loves Me' by The Smiths and Morrissey singing about love's false alarm. Once I think of knocking and going in, trying to say something that might comfort but I don't know what it would be and so I pass on by, switch off the landing light, leaving only the one in the porch as the last in the house, a light that will burn until the morning.

Lorna thinks he's struck up a friendship with a girl on his university course because she was snooping on his Facebook page and saw some photos of them. But he's never spoken of her and so his mother can't mention her because he'd know she was snooping. And that's a parental crime that comes close to every child's idea of a capital offence. It's a mystery to me that they want to pass through life without oversight or monitoring and yet leave a trail across virtual space like scattered debris so that someone with the time and inclination can piece it back together the way they reassemble those planes after a disaster. But I suggest to Lorna that it's not always a good thing to do because if they find out then everything gets made private and sometimes the fragmented pieces you're trying to reassemble have something missing and form an impression that is probably distorted and produces nothing but concern. I tell Lorna that if this nameless girl becomes important in Luke's life he'll let us know so she shouldn't go dropping hints or asking questions that will arouse his suspicion and we agree that all she's going to say is that if he ever wants to invite anyone home to stay with us during the holidays then there'd be no problem. No problem at all and she's promised that she won't even suggest she's talking about a girl.

The snow is still falling but it feels merely like the left-over remnants of the previous days and there is a lack of conviction in its half-hearted drop and sometimes the wind catches it and almost turns it round as if deciding it doesn't want any more of it covering the earth. I try to imagine what it must have been like to be holed up in one of the forts built into the wall, what it was like to stand on the ramparts with the wind sleeting in against your face and stare into the distant darkness. Coast to coast – that's a wall. Some day I'll go to look at it – maybe on the return journey after I've left Luke back at the start of a new term – because I want to understand how you build a wall, how you keep out the darkness. But what is it you need? It can't be as simple as money because even the rich fall victim to invasion and when a French priest has his throat cut in his own church it can't be divine protection. I try to offer up the possibility that it's karma but get into a mental mess trying to equate the relationship between past actions and future consequences. As I pass a stretch of land at the side of the road where the snow is inexplicably pockmarked and stamped, as if by the incessant march of heavy feet that appear to arrive from nowhere and lead nowhere, I hear Daniel's voice. And I'm not sure where it's coming from and whether it's in the satnav, the spaces in between the music or the very pores of my skin. I don't know and at first it's whispering so I can hardly hear it but then the words become clearer.

And he's talking about Luke and how we're always killing the fatted calf for him and how is that fair and why are the scales always tipped out of balance.

He's not the prodigal son, I rush at him. He's not the prodigal son and you are the one who went away from us and we always wanted you to come back and every night we left the chain off the front door and your mother put warmth in your bed on winter nights so don't try to make us feel guilty about your brother because we don't love him more or less than you. And we've always felt that, even when it was hard and our love wasn't wanted, so don't try to lay that guilt on us because we can't take it and won't take it and we tried to come to you, tried more than you will ever know or understand, and yes we'd have laid on a banquet to welcome you so don't tell yourself that only Luke matters because it isn't true it isn't true and you shouldn't say it is because it's easy to say things that are meant to hurt but we can't have any more hurt than we have right now and just after when I thought Luke was going to go under because maybe he wanted to be with his big brother it filled us with the worst fear that we've ever known so that was the very last thing you gave us after everything we gave you and sometimes I think the fear is permanent like it's stamped indelibly somewhere deep in our DNA and no matter what we do or will do in the future we'll never be free of it can you understand that can you understand?

But there is no answer and the scud of the wipers telling me that the snow has stopped falling replaces the whispering. As always after, I feel a cold emptiness I want to shake off. Perhaps it's when I try to free myself from the chill of my thoughts, the memories that don't help, that makes me drive on past until in some mental double take what I've just seen registers in my consciousness – the car tracks off the road, the broken fence, the red lights blinking – and I bring the car to a stop, stare vainly in my side mirror for what together these things mean. Then I switch on my hazard lights, get out and walk back towards the tracks to find a car has gone off the road, ploughed through a wooden fence and slid down face forward into the gully that borders the wood. There is a woman in the car, maybe my age, maybe a few years older, and her driver's airbag has inflated so it looks for a moment as if her head is resting on a drift of snow. I start to clamber down the ditch but lose my footing and slide to the bottom.

She turns her unmarked face very slowly towards me and smiles, almost as if she recognises me and has been expecting me. There is a smell from the car – of its exhaust, overheated brakes or something else that's stressed or spilt – and it's mixed with the sharp tang of the pine trees.

'Are you all right?' I ask, coming close and resting my hand on the car's roof after glancing at the crumpled bonnet.

'I think so but my left leg doesn't feel right and my neck's a bit sore. Can you help me out of here?'

'You mustn't move. I'll phone for help. You need to stay still in case you've damaged something. I'll call an ambulance and the emergency services. We'll get you out soon.'

But I've left my phone in the car and, telling her again not to move, scramble back up the bank, the snow cold against my palms.

'You'll not leave me,' she calls and as I reach the top of the bank I tell her no, that I'll make the call and be straight back.

As I run to the car my feet scrunch the frozen snow and sometimes sink below the surface so I try to move more quickly, somehow make myself lighter, but as I get closer the snow seems less willing to bear my weight and I end up running on the road, every step slushed with water. I grab the phone and check I've still got a signal and make the call. But I'm unsure about exactly where I am. The woman on the other end is patient, asking me the last place I remember, and I have to check on the satnav before I'm able to give an answer. They'll be there as soon as they can and then I grab my coat and a bottle of water, lift the sleeping bag out of the boot and run back the way I've come. And, although it's selfish, an awareness that I'm going to be delayed in getting to Luke edges into my concern for the woman.

There isn't any effective or dignified way of going back down the slope so I simply sit down and slide to the bottom.

'Thank you,' she says, as if she thought I might just have driven away.

'How are you feeling now?' I ask.

'Not so bad. My knee hurts a bit but I think I'm pretty much OK.'

'I've phoned the emergency services and they'll be here as soon as they can. What's your name?'

'Rosemary.'

'Mine's Tom.'

'Hi, Tom.'

'What happened?'

'I think I took the bend too quickly and then hit the brakes too hard. When I did that the car took on a life of its own and the next thing I'm going for a walk in the woods. Very, very stupid of me.'

'It could have happened to anyone – you've just been unlucky. The conditions aren't great.'

'I should have been more careful, less in a rush. And it's almost Christmas – what a stupid time to have an accident.'

'We aren't given a choice when our accidents happen,' I tell her and she looks at me as if she's seeing me for the first time.

'Your accent isn't local. Are you from Scotland?'

'Northern Ireland. I'm on my way to bring my son home – he's at uni in Sunderland. I came across in the boat this morning, getting it back later tonight. We were scared of him not being able to get a flight home.'

'I'm sorry I'm holding you back. You've a long journey ahead of you.'

'It's OK,' I tell her and I look at her for the first time.

She has blue eyes that seem to have some of their colour drained away by time or what her life has brought her. Her hair is cut short in a kind of bob and it's dyed blonde but there are fine grey hairs sieving through it and her face looks like it's struggling a little against the years' encroachment. But it's a face with kindness in it and a vividness of life that makes it easy to help her. Her raised hands make it look as if she's surrendering or inviting the trees to come to her.

'Do you think the car's a write-off?' she asks.

'Pretty much, I'm afraid,' I say, looking at the crumpled bonnet that from time to time emits a creak or a kind of mechanical moan as if it's trying to painfully stretch itself back into its original shape.

'Then that's the only good thing will come out of this because I always hated it,' she says but her smile turns

93

suddenly to a grimace and her eyes close briefly. I know she's in pain.

'They'll be here soon,' I tell her and turn my head towards the road in the hope of hearing the for-once welcome sound of a siren.

'I feel a bit sleepy, and that's not good, so it isn't.'

'No, so just keep talking to me, Rosemary.'

I place the unzipped sleeping bag carefully around her shoulders and, seeing her eyes close again, crouch beside her at the open door and ask her where she was going when she had the crash. I can't remember all the first-aid things you're supposed to do in a situation like this and although I search frantically in my memory it comes back empty so I don't know if I should get her to drink something but decide better not to.

'I was going to the church hall to help get it ready for tonight. It's the carol service and our school choir are performing. I'm a teacher. Chairs and photocopied carol sheets to put out. You can't be a teacher without putting out chairs. There's a box of winter holly and decorations in the boot that need putting up. Would it be all right if a teacher swears?'

When I tell her yes she hisses the word 'shit' several times, which sounds as if it's carried on a stream of frustration and anger, then apologises but I'm glad the emotion has galvanised her into alertness. Then we lapse into a moment's silence and stare at the trees and the spindrift that falls from their branches when the wind stirs them.

There is a sudden cold sweep of stillness amongst the trees that feels absolute and which seems to reach right to the very edge of us.

'Can you ring some people for me?' she asks and then when I take out my phone tells me that she doesn't know the numbers so I must use hers. 'It's in my pocket nearest to you if you could find it.'

I carefully slip my hand into her pocket and root around until I find the phone. When the screen opens there's a photograph of her and two young women who look like her daughters. Their heads are close, their affection and happiness pressing them close together, and for the first time I think a selfie can be a good thing. She gives me the access code and I go into her contacts, find the first name she wants me to dial then hold the phone close to her so she can speak into it. She's calling a colleague and explaining that she's had an accident, playing down its seriousness but saying that she'll probably be taken to hospital as a precaution, telling her that she'll try to get someone to deliver the carol sheets. Apologising several times. And then she asks me to click into her favourites and call her daughter Emily but it goes to voicemail and she doesn't leave a message.

'Emily's a nurse and she's probably on the ward. I don't want to get wheeled into hospital and for her to see me without any warning. What should I do?'

'I'll phone the hospital,' I tell her. 'Let them know that it's important to speak to her.'

I look up the number and as I'm dialling it a stronger wind brushes through the trees and releases more of their scent. I'm listening to an automated system trying to direct me to the right number and I'm confused because none of the options seems to offer the possibility of telling one of their nurses that her mother's had an accident and Rosemary anticipates what's happening and tells me to go into her pocket once more and this time find her purse. In it she's got a card with a direct line to the ward where Emily should be working. Before I ring it she says my name and when I look at her she's trying not to cry and she asks if I'll explain to her daughter and try to do it without frightening her. That if she speaks to her she thinks she'll probably cry and then they'll both get upset. I tell her I understand and make the call. There is a couple of minutes' delay and then Emily comes on the line.

'Hello, Emily,' I say, 'I'm ringing on behalf of your mother. First of all she's OK, she's OK and probably just needs a bit of a check-up. She's had a bit of an accident in the car – no, she's OK, she's going to be all right. Her leg hurts a bit but she doesn't think it's anything serious. We're just waiting for some help to arrive. Yes, I'm with her.'

When I look at Rosemary she's nodding as if to tell me that I'm doing it right and then she gestures to bring the phone close.

'Hi, Emily,' she says, her voice suddenly inflated with cheerfulness. 'I've been a bit of a dozy-head and put the car off the road. No, I'm OK. Just tweaked my knee a bit so I wanted to let you know before they wheeled me in as your next patient. I suppose if they take me to A&E I'll be sitting for hours and hours with all those poor old people who've ventured out and slipped. At least there shouldn't be late-night drunks to contend with. No, there's no need to phone Julia and get her all worried. I'll ring her when I've seen someone at the hospital and there's something to tell her. Yes, all right, and maybe you'll be able to nip down and see me in one of your breaks. OK, Emily, and don't be worrying – I'll be home to cook that turkey.'

Before I put the phone back in her pocket she makes me enter my number in her contacts so that she can thank me even though I assure her it isn't necessary. And when I ask her again how she's feeling she tells me her knee hurts but that things could have been so much worse so maybe after all she's been lucky. I think how close I was to driving on by, focused on the world inside my head, but say nothing. She asks me about Luke and what course he's doing and I keep it simple by letting her think he is our only child and then I get her to tell me about her daughters, conscious that I didn't make a phone call to a partner.

'Emily's in her second year on the wards. She likes it but it's tiring and she doesn't know how long she'll stay with it. She hates her A&E shifts – not enough doctors on duty, not enough beds and too many drunks clogging up the system. Once she had to take a blood sample and this guy made a complaint that she had got some blood on his designer shirt. Sometimes she talks about working abroad though it looks like Brexit might have damaged that possibility as far as Europe is concerned.'

'Damaged all our children's prospects, if you ask me,' I say.

'Almost all the North-east voted to leave – sixty-one per cent in Sunderland. Newcastle by a small margin to remain. Broke my heart.'

'Because we live in Northern Ireland we can get Irish passports. So at least we can get free access to travel. And your other daughter?'

'Julia is doing an internship – paid, thankfully, even if not very well – with a fashion magazine in London. She's due home tomorrow. I want to be there for her, don't want her coming home to an empty house. Are you not going to ring Luke and let him know you've been delayed a bit and tell him I'm sorry?'

I say I'll do it soon but don't want to risk his exasperation within earshot of her so put it off for the moment. We both don't want our children to be in empty houses and for one crazy second I feel the impulse to tell this stranger everything, to make this ditch that leads into a silent wood my confessional, because without knowing her I think she might understand and whatever penance she chose to offer would come with the possibility of forgiveness, and rightly or wrongly I feel that, in this frozen suspended moment where we both wait for the future to arrive, there's nothing separating us. We'll never be here again and whatever words are spoken will be subsumed into the silent snow-filled spaces that lace the trees. I remember the old black-and-white silent film about the Mallory expedition and one of the final captions that said if we had lived and died in the heart of nature would we wish for any better grave than a pure white grave of snow. If only I could put this thing in that pure white grave of snow. It makes me shiver. I look at her and she looks at me.

'Are you all right, Tom? You look cold.'

'Perhaps I should go and wait on the road so they know where we are,' I say, because I'm frightened of the words spooling on my lips.

'Don't leave me,' she says, 'please don't leave me.'

She reaches out her hand and I don't know if it's what she means but I take it and at first the touch is cold but slowly seeps into warmth. Then we both let go and for a second I think I hear the approach of an ambulance but I'm mistaken and suddenly I see her smile.

'What's so funny?' I ask.

'It's stupid, really stupid, but the choir were to sing this new piece tonight. We've been practising it for weeks because it's quite tricky and it's not even a carol really. It's an arrangement of the Robert Frost poem "Stopping by Woods on a Snowy Evening" – you know the one:

'Whose woods these are I think I know.
His house is in the village though;
He will not see me stopping here
To watch his woods fill up with snow.

'And ends:

'The woods are lovely, dark and deep,
But I have promises to keep,
And miles to go before I sleep,
And miles to go before I sleep.'

I nod because, although I couldn't recite it as she has done, it's lodged somewhere in my memory from schooldays.

'When I chose it I never thought I'd end up acting it out,' she says and she gives a little laugh which is edged with something harder. 'Life has a way of pulling the rug out from under you. At least I'll be able to make a joke about it.'

Then she winces again as if the laughter has stirred some new release of pain. I hear a siren – still in the distance but I've definitely heard it – and I tell her they're coming.

'I feel such a fool. I'm going to be really embarrassed when they get here.'

And as she blows another stream of air I tell her not to be, that it could have happened to anyone, and I describe my first attempt to set out on this journey. The siren gets louder and I persuade her I should go up to the road to guide them and she nods her agreement. So I clamber up the slope once more and step in the messed-up snow that marks my path until I reach the road in time to flag down the ambulance. Not far behind is a fire engine and suddenly there is a team of men and women swarming down the bank towards the car. The paramedics go in first and ascertain her injuries, ask me some questions, then put her in a neck brace and I overhear two firemen saying that it doesn't look as if they'll have to use cutting equipment but they can't winch the car while she's still in it. There are constant messages coming through their radios and the vehicle lights spin blue shadows across the snow. A stretcher appears and after about ten minutes when the paramedics have finished their initial assessment they start to ease her out of the car and on to it and the firefighters shoulder it delicately and carefully, easing her up the slope step by slow step, and when she passes me she calls a thanks and I raise my hand in farewell, then they have her in the back of the ambulance and she's gone. I answer some more questions from the police who have arrived, give them my name and address, and at first they think I have been a witness to the accident until I explain. And yes, I tell them, I'm on my way to Sunderland to bring my son home from uni. They thank me for my help, wish me luck and I'm free to go.

Miles to go before I sleep and time to make up but any desire to drive much faster is quashed by the image of her car nose down in the ditch. I hope she's OK and that she doesn't have to stay in hospital over Christmas, that her daughter doesn't come home to an empty house. It's stupid but I think I should have offered to deliver the carol sheets because now, more than ever, trying to do the right thing seems as important as anything else that exists, and maybe the right thing is just all the small things that one person's life can muster. But there is another voice telling me that delivering carol sheets isn't a meaningful step to any form of atonement and only a distraction from what really matters, which is to bring my son safely home.

I want to understand what it was that took Daniel ever closer to the edge. When I retake that journey I try to find a different and unmarked path, step in some new direction driven by the hope that I might end up with better answers. I mute the satnav because this part of the journey is straight and clear and because I don't want her voice, don't want her listening in case there are things I find myself able to say, and because perhaps if I try really hard it'll be Daniel's voice not hers I hear and we'll be able to talk even once like father and son or at least in a way that we've never done before. So put Rosemary's car back on the road, rewind time and start with a clean sheet, a wiped slate, the moment before images are indelibly printed. The moment that lies below the surface of things and before things happen.

He was always a surprise, born in the same year as our wedding, and this isn't easy to say and has never slipped outside the silent confines of thought but there were times when I wondered if I was his father because my anxious imagination can construct a range of bad scenarios, all of them involving Johnston Bailey. And maybe

I've tried to use this as an escape route, an abdication of responsibility. Because if this were true then there is the possibility of genetics, of an alternative DNA-printed predetermination being able to shoulder the blame. But it's a cheap thought and it shames me so much that I open the window and punish myself with the rush of cold air against my face and drive like that for a distance before I close it again. And sometimes I think of Joseph, the father-to-be of a child who isn't his, and it doesn't really matter much about what his wife has told him because nothing she says can make any sense and when the Angel appears to him in a dream how can he trust what he remembers in the cold light of day without wondering if he has only imagined what he wanted to hear? So Mary becomes the heroine, the holy object of veneration, and Joseph fades into the shadows for ever. But I remember enough to recall that the story describes him as a good man and, although we have no way of knowing if he was a good father to this child who wasn't fully ever his, I believe he must have been, even if he finally came to believe the Angel's words and in so doing was separated for ever from any sense of flesh of his flesh. So if we could, I think we should bring him out of those shadows and make him part of this celebration of a child born in a manger, let some of the lights that decorate our homes burn for him.

Daniel resists coming into the world for so long that the doctor thinks they'll have to operate but perhaps the prospect of the scalpel is the only thing that's ever seemed to frighten him because almost immediately he appears. Dark of hair and eye, he's quick to let us know his lungs are working and the nurses joke about it as they clean him and hand him to Lorna and she quite rightly refuses a photograph and is irritated by my insensitivity.

'I don't want a photograph of me looking a mess,' she tells me. 'There'll be plenty of time later and why not just look at him with your eye for once and not through the camera.'

And a few minutes later she gives me him and I feel the inexplicable confusion of holding your first child and struggling to understand your connection with this new life and your responsibility for it. So if an angel were to appear and say this being you cradle in your arms has come from the Holy Spirit it would make as much sense as anything else in that moment. But look at him with your eye. He's plump-cheeked with small dark pupils, his skin crinkled like wet paper, his face as if shrink-wrapped. The hands are most incredible, sculpted perfect and made from still-wet clay so when I touch one with my finger I'm frightened it might puddle out of shape and then they tighten on mine and nothing has ever felt like that before or since. And he's born in July, the time of marching and beating drums, of arguing about who owns one road or another and the lighting of huge fires with their pallets and toxic fumes from tyres. When I leave the hospital late at night the air is acrid with smoke sliming itself on the back of the throat and the sky is black-brushed with twisting plumes that make me remember things from the past that I don't want to intrude on this special moment. The sirens of fire engines wail through the streets and once glimpsed between houses near Sandy Row is a yellow and blue thresh of flame throwing its quiver against the silhouettes of taller buildings. The city becomes a giant shadow play with wavering images printed on gable walls and although it's supposed to be celebratory everything is edged with a sense of menace that makes me press the button that locks the car's doors. And I hope my son is safely cradled in his mother's arms far from these sounds and the carcinogens that spiral from the burning tyres and the still-smouldering hatreds.

Of course there are photographs, more than we ever took of our other two children because that's what it's like with a first child. Everything has to be recorded in some evolutionary chronicle, as if a missed moment will leave a blank in our parental memory, but I rarely look at them now and each of the different phases has blurred so I can't distinguish any more where each one started and ended. All the inevitable clichés are contained in those same photographs – the blowing out of the birthday candles; the first paddle in the sea; posed at our front door with plastic lunch box in hand for the first day of school. A clever child, instinctively smarter than Luke could ever be, who did really well in school at the start before industry was needed to complement what came naturally. And I can't think of Daniel as that child without freeing him from whatever stillness he has found now and setting him spinning in some new motion. So I see him climbing, always in air, the bars of the cot merely a challenge, and then it was trees, and roofs, the park pavilion where he tagged his name and once on holiday a tunnel over the railway line close to where we stayed. And Lorna tells me we can't punish a child because he has no fear and so our concern is edged with an unspoken pride but if I can go back I'll tell him that it's not good to have no fear, that it's dangerous not to feel it. Because that's what makes him reckless all his life. Tell him that it's wrong to trust so fully the insubstantial vagaries of air, the unpredictable whims of balance. And where does this come from because it's not part of his mother, and I am someone averse to risks, in recent days tormented by the recurring dream where I walk far out on that frozen lake, waiting with each new step for it to crack.

'So where does it come from, Daniel?' I ask but he can't be summoned any more than he can be bent to my will or anyone else's. And there is only the sound of the slush under the car's wheels and the fine spray from the white van in front that makes me switch on the wipers but I hesitate and for a moment peer darkly at the world through the spotted windscreen. Then I clear it to see a tractor in a field and a farmer pitching fodder from the trailer. On the television local news there have been stories of farmers looking for their missing sheep, hardened men with furrowed weather-beaten faces suddenly confronted with a loss that is obviously more than economic, and one finding a ewe still living, surviving in a drift against a stone wall because it's found an air pocket, his dog barking and skittering excitedly round his feet as he wields the spade and then with one final heft pulls its black bewildered face free. And if I had been a better father I would have found my son while there was still time, pulled him out. This is what I know and can't unknow however much I want to. Crows drift slow-winged above the tractor in the hope that there might be something left for them to scavenge. Where did those bats fleeing from our smoke and darkly stuttering into the night air find a new refuge? Somehow on that night of his birth as I drove away from the hospital the beat of their wings blurred with the trails churning the sky but now I know that it wasn't so and it was only after what happened that these two events were spliced together. And that's one of the most difficult things as I try to think because time no longer stays ordered and chronological like the photographs I took of his growth into childhood and instead jumps back and forward, later events supposedly signalled by earlier ones to which I was oblivious at the time because what I'm always seeking is a pattern to impose on the chaos. And there's a kind of attempted internal photoshopping with something deliberately erased because it stings like a paper cut each time you let your mind touch it and other things that get enhanced with meaning that was probably never there in the first place or because the memory allows you to invest some claim to goodness or transfer blame elsewhere.

Lorna and I have never blamed each other, sharing it equally, even sometimes temporarily taking it from the other's shoulders when the burden gets too heavy, and we have little sequences of phrases that by now are almost like a learned script which serve as lifelines to try and stop us going under. And we know we can't go under because we have Lilly and Luke still to care for. But there are moments too when the lifelines don't reach and we fall into a ritual of almost competitive self-accusation, then try to escape where that leads us by finding other things, other people to blame. This is the worst time for me because I find myself echoing what she says when I know that if I were a stronger and better person I would tell her the truth and take the consequences but I can't do that because I've already lost too much and I can't risk losing any more.

I pass trees dusted lightly with snow that look as if they have simply shrugged off the heavier falls; children in a field sledging their favoured route on the slope until it's polished shiny; a lorry parked up at the roadside with a wavering haze off its engine and slops of snow melting off its bodywork. And I tell myself that I'll do it after Christmas, that whatever the risks I have to do it, try to find the right words so that she might just be able to understand that anything I did I did because I thought it was right and wanted nothing more than to protect all of us. But the prospect frightens me and I feel a need to talk to Luke, to know he's all right and to tell him that I'm on my way, that I might even have done the worst of the journey.

He answers right away and asks me if everything's OK so for a second I feel panicked and wonder if he is able to sense what I'm thinking and feeling.

'Everything's fine,' I tell him. 'I got a bit delayed by an accident but I'm still on course.'

'Was it serious?'

'Not too bad, someone came off the road and slipped into the ditch.'

'So are the roads still bad?'

'The main ones are pretty well-cleared and the traffic has churned them into mostly slush but the side roads still look pretty rough.'

'But you'll be staying on main roads, won't you?'

'Yes, all the way. Do you remember you once asked me why we call the seaside the seaside when it might be the front or the back?'

'No,' he says and the tone of his voice suggests it's just a story I've made up to embarrass him so I let it go. 'I've been listening to The Great Lake Swimmers CD you gave me for my birthday and I think it's very good.'

'That's good. Glad you like it.'

'And how're you feeling?'

'Not so bad. I'll be glad to get home but I'm not looking forward to the boat. I don't want to end up hooping. Was it rough when you came over?'

'Really smooth. It'll be fine.'

'So how much longer, do you think, before you get here?'

'About an hour. Stay warm and I'll text you when I'm there,' I say and I almost add, 'Just like when I picked you up at Amber's house,' but I don't. 'And, Luke, give your mum a call, let her know that I'm not that far away and that you're feeling a bit better. And you'll be pleased to know that she's given me every medicine and pill in the house for you to take.'

'I've already had my instructions by text.'

'No doubt in great detail.'

This shared, pretend exasperation at Lorna's insistent mothering creates a sense of closeness between us but underneath we both know we're grateful and feel protected by it. When the call is finished I drive a little quicker but within the limits of safety and wonder what we'll talk about on the return journey and wonder too if we'll ever talk about Daniel. It's never happened and I don't know whether trying to make it happen would be a good or bad thing but I decide it would be wrong to force it and so should wait until he's ready to talk, whenever that might be. And anyway the other thing I don't know is what I will say, just as I didn't know what to say that night when he was in his room after Amber had broken up with him, and I need to be sure of it before the moment arrives. It's not helped by never really knowing what Luke's thinking and afterwards he drew into a deeper privacy of self, on the surface almost detached from the external events that we had to give ourselves to, and if we asked him if he was all right he'd get annoyed and retreat behind the shut door of his room. It was the silence coming from it that I found hard to bear because if as always there had been the sound of music I would have known from his choices what was going on in his head. But there was nothing, just that unfamiliar, uncharacteristic silence and the shut door keeping us out and impossible to enter no matter how much we wanted to.

Daniel first left home when he was eight. He had campaigned for a dog but with both of us out working all day we decided against it, told him that we'd consider it when he was older and able to look after it. But even then he was an instant child, short of the patience that so much of life needs, his low levels of concentration making him flit from one thing to another and no matter how much we worked with him that never really changed. So he wanted a dog but we guessed that in a short while he'd lose interest in it and have moved on to something else. But he took it badly, assuring us repeatedly of the commitment he'd make to it, how he'd walk and feed it, do everything that a good owner should, and how we'd benefit too because it would be a guard dog and so we'd never be burgled. He also enlisted Luke's support for his cause. When it was clear that his persuasion hadn't worked he took off, leaving a note saying he was going to get his own dog. We found him in the kids' playground in the park, sitting on the top of a slide complete with a dog lead whose origin we never discovered and his face set in an attempted sullen mask but unable to hide his relief at seeing us. The desire for a dog came and went just like we thought it would.

However, we came to see our child's capacity for being … I don't know if this is the right word but it might be headstrong. A strange word. When you think about it, it should be something good, a marker of internal strength, but when we use it we're thinking of stubborn, self-willed, someone who acts without enough thought.

Reckless, I suppose.

I turn on the satnav – I don't want to lose my way when I'm getting ever closer and heading for that never-ending sequence of ring roads. Want to hear a voice telling me which one to take because I need that now. Someone with a poor grasp of consequences – that's probably how we started to think of Daniel. Sometimes I look intently at Lilly and there've been moments when she catches me and wants to know what I'm looking at and I say something like, 'My best girl,' or if she's screwing up her face, 'I don't know but it's looking back at me,' but I'm really trying to see if there's any trace of the future in her face, to see if there's anything that should cause us worry. Something that could be prevented. At school almost everything gradually went to hell for Daniel just at the time when it was important that he got things right. Only his art survived the slide and in part I think that was due to his teacher – the same Mrs Clark who taught Luke. She believed in him and I'm grateful for that and when he'd have been happy to walk away she coaxed him, nagged him, persuaded him to complete the course, and she'd never get flustered, more likely to laugh at some of his antics than get cross. She never ran out of patience and you can't ask anything more than that from a teacher. Afterwards she sent me some of his work, seeking our permission to keep a couple of pieces that she was particularly fond of. Sometimes parents donate cups as expressions of gratitude or tributes to departed ones but it would have embarrassed the school to have a Prize Day award with Daniel's name on it so in the end we simply sent her a thank-you card and at the last moment I included a copy of the photograph I'd taken on his first day.

We've looked at his work a lot. On occasions together, sometimes on our own. Once I found Lorna on her knees in his room, her hands moving lightly over everything as if it was a form of braille and through her touch she might read whatever it was she thought she might find there. There's sketchbooks and work on different themes that he never showed us but the central piece is three portraits of an old man – Mrs Clark got them framed and they were good enough to be shown in the examination board's end-of-year exhibition. He never went with us to look at them, never saw our pride. The first in this series of three is a realistic portrait of the man sitting in his armchair; the second has the same face but with a slightly different expression and his head is surrounded by a photoshopped collage that represents his memories and they seem to be good ones, particularly of childhood. The third darkens the face and perhaps it's fear flecking his eyes and this time the collaged images are disturbing – a headstone, a woman crying, a house in flames. I look at them a lot but try to resist the urge to read things into them, to twist the images to fit whatever interpretation currently occupies my thoughts. Sometimes I think the old man has the look of my father and so perhaps just a little like me but Lorna tells me I'm imagining it and I'm happy to believe her.

And if we were to make a collage of your childhood, Daniel, there'd be lots of good things with which to halo

your head and at intervals I reignite their memory and try
to stir some warmth. But today there is no time for this
and I try only to identify the start and that isn't the same as
when Lorna and I first knew we were losing you because
it must have come before that. But maybe not even you
know the when, the where and the how, any more than
you were able to give a reason for anything that happened, almost as if things just did happen without reason
or meaning and you were mostly a spectator, a bemused
bystander to your own life. And you'd sometimes smile
and shrug your shoulders as if they were unknowable or
had only some vague connection with you and so you
weren't ever fully responsible for them. And you always
had the advantage of what gets called charm, a lightness in
your eyes, so your face never held that sullen expression
beloved by teenagers. It was only much later when you
were fully committed, when you were in over your head
and powerless to step back into who you once were, that
you'd stop smiling and it's one of the saddest things that
the time when you had the greatest awareness of what
was happening was also when you had least ability to save
yourself. Maybe just like those two men who fell through
the frozen air with everything locked in that final motion
and hands powerless to find a hold. And I sometimes think
that I or anyone else couldn't save you, couldn't find you
and pull you free, because you weren't able to let me or
let Lorna do any of the things that might have made that
possible. But this thought gets blighted by the image of
the farmer never giving up and digging with his spade to
the sound of the dog's barking and how with his hands
sunk deep he pulls the black-faced sheep from its burial
place. Sometimes I try to tell myself that it was because

you loved us both that you held yourself apart, stayed hidden, or that you wanted us to think of you as you once were, but I find no conviction either in this attempt at comfort because by the end I know you weren't able to think of anyone else: not me, not your mother and especially not yourself.

Why did you need it? In my time I've needed different things but mostly love to ward off loneliness and the sadness to which I now know I'm vulnerable. But never even for a moment did I ever think I would find this thing I craved in anything except another person so I struggle to grasp what prompts those who think so differently.

And what I want from my body is to stay as focused and balanced enough to see me through each of my days so the thought of willingly taking anything that might affect this just fills me with confusion.

'Why do you need it?' I asked once in one of those last conversations I tried to have.

'I don't need it,' you answered with all the smiling self-delusion of the person who thinks they don't need help because they're in control. And in the end that's what destroyed you because right from the earliest times – the experiments with the sometimes legal and before the final slide and fall – you always believed you could hold your balance, stay sure-footed. Walk that high wire and never ever slip.

Now I think I should have asked instead, 'What is it you need?' because if you had known the answer to that then we could have tried to find it and there's nothing we wouldn't have done to help that search. But what if it wasn't that you believed you'd never fall but that you no longer cared if you did? I can't think of that without journeying into a realm of suffering that will produce collateral damage so I turn away from it.

Lies and absences become the pattern of our days. Lorna hates a lie because she has this strict moral sense that can't help but be angered by this intentional deviation from the truth. I never feel the right to judgement because I know that lies are mostly just things we tell to avoid either pain to ourselves or someone else. But I also know that their consequences are unpredictable and we have no way of controlling where it will lead us in the end. It's of other things, however, that I am mindful when we're sitting with you in the police station. It's the first time I've ever been in one and you're sixteen and we wait in a seating area that has the feel of an A&E department with its plastic chairs, bruised surfaces with a preponderance of black scuff marks from trainers, and posters that exhort us to report various crimes such as domestic abuse and remind us of a range of civic responsibilities. There is one from a charity with a suicide-prevention telephone number and as we sit with a group of other people who avoid eye contact with each other I think that it really is an alternative A&E and most of the people who come here are damaged in some way and in need of care.

And Lorna and I are hopeful that we're going to get it because we've not done well recently and when you break the rules we make, cross the boundaries we've tried to set, we don't have any meaningful punishment that we can bring to bear on a sixteen-year-old. So we're feeling a little helpless and unsure of what to do about your lies and absences. Of the way even then you've started to use your home as a stopover that you no longer invest anything of yourself in, that you're always passing through. So here we sit waiting for you to encounter a higher authority and receive a formal warning for underage drinking and anti-social behaviour. And I don't know if we're more upset by the drinking or the fact that you thought it was just a bit of fun to throw eggs at an old-age pensioner's house who had the temerity to tell you off for the disturbance you were creating. And what your mother and I need more than anything is to see something in you that resembles remorse and if we can't see that then we want there to be the fear that coming face to face with the police should engender.

I look at your expression but can't read anything and I want to shake you when you start playing with your mobile phone but Lorna tells you to put it away with a sharpness in her voice that makes some of the waiting heads turn.

There's a man in motorcycle leathers, his helmet on his wrist like a bracelet; a mirrored couple who are equally badly overweight and wearing matching grey tracksuits where even the stains seem synchronised; an older man who holds a letter in a way that makes it seem as if he's offering a public explanation for his presence; and a young woman permanently on her phone with what looks like a black eye under heavy make-up. The police who come into the station throw us all a disinterested, cursory glance before they disappear down a corridor. The officer at the desk acknowledges them with the briefest nod and does his best not to make eye contact with any of us.

Eventually we get called and shown into an interview room where a policewoman young enough to be your sister asks if she can call you Danny and you say yes even though we think she should call you Daniel and then calmly outlines the future consequences of your actions, the potential implications for career and life prospects, but it's not what we want. We both look at each other with disappointment because we know that it's not journeying anywhere further than your surface so all your nodding of your head and serious face might fool her but we've seen it assumed before and don't buy into it. But what is it we wanted from this talk? For her to shout and show you the hangman's rope? For her to take you by the throat and shake you into some better sense of yourself and responsibility to others? I don't know but as we drive home in silence I understand fully for the first time that there's no help coming and everything is down to us, then when Lorna and I are in bed that night we try to tell ourselves that it's a phase that lots of kids go through and hard as it is you'll come out the other side and everything will be all right. Everything will work out all right. Everything will work out all right in the end. It's a kind of refrain we sing to each other, something to lull us into an easier sleep.

But it's never all right and even if you don't bring them round very often I don't know who these new friends are except they're not kids from school and although I try not to be judgemental I don't like the look of them. And you're asking me when I first knew you were taking? The start of the summer some weeks after you'd left school for the last time and I came down in the night to find you in the kitchen. I sleep light so I heard you coming in and when you looked at me I just knew. It was something in your eyes, something different to everything that had gone before, as if you were seeing me in some way that was altered and that there was something separating us that travelled beyond the normal distance between father and son. And I was so frightened that I couldn't even ask you because if I had and you had lied I would have known for sure and in that moment I didn't know how to deal with that. I guess you knew that I saw because you started staying over with friends more often, coming home to sleep and change your clothes. Coming home to steal.

Lorna has searched your room, gone through it with a fine-tooth comb but found nothing, even though like me she knows nothing about drugs and might not even recognise anything she discovered, but I think she knows better than anyone with a mother's instinctive awareness of changes in her child's appearance, changes in appetite and routine. And your possessions of value have slowly disappeared and you tell us that you're storing them with friends because you want to share a flat in Belfast when you start at art college because you've managed to get in on the strength of your portfolio and just for a while we find in that a better hope for the future. But other things go missing as well. Things that don't belong to you. Money, and smaller objects at first that you think won't be noticed and which you can turn into cash. But none of them matters so much as what disappears in you. You hear me, Daniel: none of it mattered so much as what we lost in you. So who are you now?

Stand with me and look at yourself in the mirror. See your sallow skin and see yourself thinner so your clothes hang on you, and your eyes – the one thing you can never hide – red-rimmed, pupils shrunk, and despite your weight loss it's as if your body is a burden to be carried. See that there's something heavy inside you, something hidden to us but which you carry and we know is there.

The absences grow longer. You mostly don't answer our calls. We're both waiting for you one night when you do come home and we sit at the kitchen table without the light on, our cups of tea grown cold, and sometimes we hold hands for strength. When we fall into silence I hear a moth looking for admittance and fluttering against the glass, the drip of the tap, the sound of a distant car. The only light is that which filters in from the hall so you don't see us at first and jump a little when you do then take a glass and fill it with water.

'Where've you been?' Lorna asks.

'Just out with mates? What's wrong?'

'You're wrong. That's what's wrong, Daniel,' she says. 'Now sit down because we need to talk to you,' and part of me is glad that she's taking the lead. 'We can't go on like this,' she tells him. 'You coming and going and we know that you've changed and not in a good way. We think that you might be taking stuff – stuff that isn't good for you.'

'What stuff?' you ask with a half-hearted simulation of confusion that barely convinces yourself and when you shrug your shoulders I can see your skinny shoulder blades rise and fall under your T-shirt. You lift the glass to your mouth and your wrists are bony knobs.

'We're not fools, Daniel. Why don't you be truthful with us now and we'll do everything that we can do to help.'

You look at the table. I look at it too. It's the same table where we've shared a lifetime of meals, where we've played card games and homeworks have been done. It's the same solid table that has anchored us, around which we've all sat, so let it be the sounding board for truth. But you have other holy objects now and you're not ready to give them up.

'So you think I'm doing drugs, that I'm a junkie?' you ask with a better show of indignation.

'No one's saying you're a junkie. No one's saying that but you've changed and we're scared because we don't know what's going on.'

'Nothing's going on. I just go out with a few mates, have a couple of beers, play some computer games. Just like half the world.'

'If you're in trouble we want to help,' I say.

'I don't know what you're on about. A few beers isn't going to hurt anyone.'

'We're not talking about a few beers,' Lorna says. 'You've lost weight, you don't eat properly and you've changed. It doesn't feel right, Daniel.'

She stretches her hand across the table to take yours but you don't open it to hers. In that moment I think of the sculpted fingers that so enthralled me the night you were born and how they clasped mine.

'Your mum's worried. I'm worried and Lilly misses you – she's always asking where you are and when you're coming home. She really wanted you to see her in the school play.'

'What did you tell her?'

'That you had to go to the art college for an interview.'

'I'll make it up to her,' you say and I'm pleased because it feels like you mean it but I know in this moment I'll cling to any hope that's offered. And if I could I'd rewind the years until we'd be sitting round this same table and playing Happy Families and trying to make our families complete by our honest giving and taking.

You stand up and take your glass to the sink then say goodnight and leave us still sitting at the table with Lorna only able to hold back the tears until we hear your footsteps on the stairs. Absences and lies all through that summer and you hardly bother with Luke any more as you become not much more than a shadow that moves across the house and then fades into missing days. And that shadow makes the house cold, sends each of us turning into ourselves because we don't know how to be around you or even how to talk about you when you're not there. Lilly alone tries to put things into words but struggles to find them and then comes to understand that whatever is happening has to be added to the list of things for which adults don't have answers.

I think, Luke, there was a time when you looked up to him without it ever crossing into hero worship and even when that faded at the end of your teens you still stay loyal so when I try to ask you about your brother you simply shrug in a blanket disclaimer and make it obvious that you've nothing to spill, no insights you're able or willing to share. And there's not much practical help from any of the outside agencies we approach apart from the type of advice we're already familiar with from the Internet because it has to be our son who does the asking and that's not going to happen. So, Daniel, it has to begin with you and nothing is possible unless you want it. And only once do I think that might happen and it's one morning at the end of the summer when I can feel the season's first slow slippage into change and I have to go up to the North Coast to take photographs for a new tourist brochure that I've tendered for and won because I probably offered to charge about half the going rate and you ask if you can come with me. Just out of the blue you ask if you can come. And before we can stop her Lorna is almost singing and talking about making sandwiches until I persuade her not to fuss and we'll pick up something on the way. Then she understands the risk of breaking the fragility of the moment's decision and lets us go without fanfare.

We're in the car, in the car together, Daniel, and the one thing I'm not going to do is talk about anything except what you want to talk about and even if you don't want to talk it doesn't matter. So at first we just drive and then you start to look at the music available and when you find the Johnny Cash CD you laugh but I tell you it's not what you expect and I insist on playing the track 'Hurt' and it suddenly becomes sadder than anything I've ever heard and I have to look away and force myself not to cry.

And I know you're listening too but don't know what you're thinking until it's too much and I'm glad when it's over. I've never played that track again. Can never play it again in my whole life.

'We could put something more cheery on like The Smiths,' I say and you almost laugh again.

'I heard them every other night coming through Luke's wall for I don't know how many years. Misery at midnight.'

'I like them – they're a good band for a man who suffers from anxieties.'

'What anxieties?' he asks.

'Just about everything under the sun,' I say but don't expand and then regret it because it might be a way of admitting that I too am flawed and vulnerable but try to keep on going and not yield to the temptation of giving up.

You rifle through the CDs and put on The National and I say it's a good choice and you grin when I tell you that when he sings about racing like a pro now, for about a year I thought he was saying racing like a pronoun. We stop at the Dark Hedges and I try to get an atmospheric picture that doesn't include tourists, parked cars or farm machinery on the road but it's almost impossible. You take some shots with your phone and then we head to the rope bridge at Carrick-a-Rede that connects the mainland with a small island and where you need a head for heights. I'm not comfortable on the moving narrow structure but you stroll across and stop in the middle and look down as all around you Japanese tourists take selfies with their cameras and phones on sticks as if they're holding up magic wands to cast a spell over themselves. I go to take a picture of you as you walk ahead but you see me and shake your head so I don't and wait until we're both on the island then, looking back, take some shots. You ask to take one and I explain the camera, hand it over and don't want the moment to end. Then when I'm walking back and resolutely not looking down my path gets blocked by some people taking selfies and suddenly I have to get off the bridge and set my feet on solid ground so I brush past them and this time you are laughing which sounds sweeter than any music.

'So you're scared of heights,' you say back in the car as if pleased to discover a weakness.

'Not scared. Just uncomfortable. But everybody has something that scares them. Your mother can't do spiders. And when there's one in the bath I have to get it out and it's not good enough to wash it down the plughole because she says it might just climb up again.'

I try to ask about art college and if you're looking forward to it but it doesn't produce any kind of committed response and we know there's another subject in the car that squats heavily between us but about which we're not going to speak unless something happens that surprises us both. I do a couple more locations and then we stop at a chippy and eat out of the papers while sitting in the car facing the sea.

There's a group of teenagers being taught to paddle-board and some of them are struggling to stay on and tumbling into the water every few minutes.

'It must be harder than it looks,' I say.

'I always wanted to try surfing.'

'What's to stop you taking it up? You'd probably be good at it,' I tell you, hugging the idea of some future pleasure and focus. 'There's places up here that run classes, hire out boards. I can check it out for you if you like.'

But you shake your head as if even thinking of it is burdensome and then you sink lower in your seat, turn the heating higher and we head to the Giant's Causeway where I try to generate some enthusiasm for what I've always thought of as a pretty boring bunch of stones and I start to wonder why I've been asked to do this job when they could just download a lot of generic shots of something that's been photographed thousands of times. I'm trying to find some semi-original angle when I look over to where you stand on a rocky outcrop jutting out to sea and suddenly you seem unbearably small when faced with that immensity and I call your name but it gets lost in the rising wind. You put your hood up and when I see you shiver I'm steeped in an unfathomable fear, fear for you and for all of us. When you turn it's to ask if I'm nearly finished and I know the day is over and that whatever I hoped for is not going to happen.

What were you thinking when you looked at the sea? Tell me now, Daniel. Or was there nothing at all except the coldness seeping into your skin? It hurts me to think about it because I can't do it without seeing you surrounded by what felt like a loneliness that I couldn't breach. And now in my dreams when I call your name again and again my voice is drowned out by the wind and the restless sea's incessant complaint. Afterwards you don't come home but ask me to drop you off near the university on our way back through the city and I don't drive away until you've walked out of sight.

In the car the phone rings but I don't answer it. I'm not ready to talk to anyone and I've started on the more complicated part of the journey that takes me on carriageways and a series of roads and roundabouts letting me bypass Newcastle and sets me towards Gateshead. So I'm grateful for hearing your calming, directing voice once more because just for a moment it takes some of the emptiness out of the car that even the music can't fill.

Not perhaps the best photographs I've ever taken but I try to hold on to the better images of that day – both of us in the car and you walking across the bridge disdaining to hold the side rails – and I try, too, to have once more the briny tang of the sea and the smell of the fish and chips in the car, the shared music. Sometimes I imagine you surfing because I know you would have been good at it and when I bring Luke home we'll all go sledging and if the garage is still open on my return journey I'll buy another one so we can go down together. I do this a lot – try to create pictures and let them pave the way to some future happiness but they are short-lived, almost fading away as soon as they've been printed and exposed to the light because in their place are more insistent and caustic ones that seem to exist outside any exercise of my will.

So Luke is out with friends at someone's birthday party and Lorna and Lilly are at the cinema and I'm in my room lying on top of the bed because I feel a weariness that takes me beyond the desire for television or anything at all which requires concentration. I've had a long day taking photographs at a wedding where the bride and groom exude what feels almost like a hostility to each other and an even greater one to everyone else trying to make their day memorable, so I don't even bother asking anyone to smile and do everything at double speed because an irritated impatience ripples out from the happy couple and infects all around them. I should be looking at the pictures and trying to make the best of a bad job in my small studio situated in the extension at the back of the house for which we haven't finished paying yet, but I can't face it tonight and need to have shrugged off the day's dismal mood or risk darkening the start to a married life. When I'm feeling like I am in those moments, and I can see the possible start of a depression creeping slowly over the horizon, I always want to sleep, to shut down physically and mentally. Try to ward it off at the pass.

As I drive and sometimes see car tracks curving across lanes on the road I think of the woman I stopped to help. And it seems to me that what this feeling I'm thinking about is like is looking into those woods filling up with snow and wanting to walk into their depths until you disappear and can't be found, not because of the film's caption that there is no better grave than that of pure white snow, but because sometimes simply not being seems a better alternative to being and feeling. And I know that the promise I have to keep is bringing my son home and it's a good thing that I have this to galvanise me, to stop me going back to where her car crashed and vanishing in those woods.

I look at my phone. It's Lorna's number but I guess it's probably from Lilly so I pull off the road into the entrance of an industrial park and call her.

'Is that you, Lilly?'

'No, it's Lorna but it was Lilly who phoned even though I told her not to. Is everything all right?'

'Everything's good. I'm not far away now and if there's no more snow we'll be on the boat back tonight.'

'I've looked at the weather forecast lots of times but they seem to be saying it's moving south now.'

'What's the betting they get the airports open again just as I arrive?'

'I don't care, Tom. We couldn't take the risk and I'm glad you're there to bring him home. I wouldn't want him travelling on his own when he's not well. And there's always the risk that they'd see he was ill and not let him board the plane.' There is a second's silence and then she says, 'You've done really well and I'm proud of you.'

I don't know what to say so you ask me again if I'm OK and I tell you yes and trying not to feel like a fraud makes me frightened. Lilly wants to tell me a joke so you put her on.

'Knock, knock.'

'Who's there?'

'Wayne.'

'Wayne who?'

'Wayne in a manger.'

'That's your best one yet,' I say, wondering whether I should try to simulate laughter but instead I tell her, 'I'll soon be getting Luke and when we're home we'll all go sledging.'

'You've already told me that.'

'Sorry for boring you. Is the snowman still there? It hasn't melted yet, has it?'

'No it's just like when you left.'

And there is comfort in that simple assurance. Then she says a sudden goodbye and doesn't give me a chance to say anything to Lorna as the phone goes dead. Maybe she's done me a favour.

The house is empty and my head is heavy with worries and I think that if I can sleep the weariness will leach away but as I start the slow shutting down I'm aware of noise from downstairs and at first I think it's Luke or Lorna and Lilly but then realise that it's too early for them to be back. So I try to stir and reluctantly make myself return to the world I'd hoped to escape and as I finally sit up and listen there is only silence at first and I think I've imagined it. But an empty house breathes in a different way to one that is not and then I hear a door open and close downstairs and although we haven't seen him for more than two weeks I guess it's Daniel and even before I get off the bed I'm angry with him. Angry for the pain he causes us, for the tears his mother sheds, for the confusion felt by Lilly who asks us if we've done something bad to him. And for Luke who doesn't show what he's feeling.

I try to stem the anger as I go down the stairs but it floods back and suddenly I'm thinking that bringing things to a head is a less painful option than letting them drag out along this unpredictable and erratic path. That somehow trying to take control of the situation in which we find ourselves might bring us closer to a better place. But he's nowhere to be seen and I consider once again whether I've imagined his presence, that my son who takes up so much of my waking thoughts has simply formed himself from the anxieties that occupy my mind. Then I realise there's someone in the studio and I consider the possibility of whether we have a burglar and wonder should I retrace my steps and call the police. But as I stand perfectly still and listen intently I know it's Daniel in the way he presses his presence however lightly into the consciousness of the house, just as I can feel his presence in the emptiness of his room on those nights I linger in it before sleep, or in the hours around dawn when I enter to confirm what I already know – that he's not there, that he hasn't come home. I don't understand why he's in the studio and when I do, at first I try to tell myself that it can't be so, but then know there's no basis for that denial except a desire to escape the consequences.

I startle him so he hasn't time to jettison my camera or what looks like Lilly's tablet and because he's startled I should take the moment's advantage but my anger doesn't allow me to think clearly and so I shout at him and ask what the fuck he's doing.

'Nothing,' he says and in the half-light of the room his voice is almost as waif-like as his body.

'Doesn't look like nothing to me, Daniel,' I tell him with my voice still raised and wavering in anger. 'Looks like you're stealing from your family. Stealing from me and from your kid sister. Stealing from Lilly. Sneaking round our home like some cheap little thief who doesn't give a shit about anyone else except himself.'

Now I know that when I used the words 'our home' I shut him out from it and in truth that's what I meant to do because in that moment I saw his presence as something toxic, infecting the well-being of my family and which would destroy us all if we let it. And when you don't answer or attempt to justify yourself it doesn't lessen my anger but rather increases it because it's as if you can't be bothered to try and muster a defence. I rip the camera and tablet out of your hands and remember now I looked at the camera to see if it had been damaged in any way and maybe in those seconds I worried that even this too had been contaminated. I don't switch on the light because I don't want to have to see you any more clearly than I do now but even so I can see the scab that disfigures the side of your mouth and how your whole face looks as if it is crimped and pulled into a tight memory of itself. And you frighten me because you look like someone who is a half-remembered stranger and when I try to force all my memories of you into a greater sense of recognition they come up short.

'I need money,' you say and even your voice sounds different to me because it's thin and stripped of the self-confidence that helps you exercise control over the situations in which you find yourself. 'I need money to pay my rent and because I had to borrow some off a mate. I'll pay you back as soon as I get my loan for art college. It'll be here soon.'

'So you thought you'd come here and just take what you could get your hands on. What does that make you?'

'I know what it makes me. But I need the money so will you help me or not? I haven't got much time.'

It's an impatient ultimatum and my anger finds a new pulse because we both know what the money's for and yet I'm the one who's going to be in the wrong, the father who's refusing to help his son. This is the moment. This is the moment on my constant reruns when different courses of action clamour for my choice, each one presenting itself as the best, and sometimes, just for a second, I try to convince myself that it was one of these I followed. But instead you stand awkwardly, as if contracted into yourself with only the tremor in your hands that mirrors the shiver I feel inside revealing something else. Then I tell myself that I see everything clearly, that I know what is best, and so what I tell you is to get out, that you're not wanted in our home and although I don't say it I don't want you there when your mother and sister return because I know they'll come back with a shared happiness and I won't see that snatched away from them. And when you hesitate I tell you again and all the anger and fear break and course into the shout of my voice and when you slip out of the room's shadows I realise I'm shaking and so I set the camera down in case I drop it and hold on to the table for support until I'm able to calm the race of my breath and my trembling body into something that resembles stillness.

I open the car window once more and let the world breathe against my face, try to douse the burn of shame and anger. I spit swear words against the windscreen. It's not you I'm angry with any more, Daniel — I've started to understand that it's much too late for that even though there's times when it's what I still want to hold on to because when you're desperate to stay afloat you'll clutch at anything. Do you understand, Daniel? I'm not angry with you any more but the cold air rushes against my skin and drowns out any chance of hearing your voice. And I never tell Lorna what's happened and when she returns Lilly is bubbling over about the film and saying I should have gone and that if I want she'll go with me and see it again. Your mother says you're hyper with popcorn and a sugary drink that they charged an arm and a leg for but yes the film was pretty good although she wouldn't want to see it twice. Then she glances at me and asks if I'm OK and I tell her yes, just a bit tired.

'What has you so tired?' she asks and I know she's looking for signs that I'm not feeling right and I let her think that's what's wrong because it's easier that way.

'Just dipped a little. I'll be fine,' I tell her.

'Why don't you head on up and I'll get this girl organised,' she says as she combs a hand through my hair.

In the bedroom I push the door almost closed, keep the light off so the room is partly lit only by the landing light, and despite Lilly talking about seeing her film twice I haven't yet started to want a rerun with a different ending to what's just happened. So for the moment as I press my head into the pillow I think I've done the right thing and protected my family and if that's meant throwing off what felt most dangerous to its survival then it's a price that has to be paid. Every noise in the house seems sharp-edged and I pull the duvet higher on my head to try to blunt them as last of all I hear you doing what I normally do as you check the front door and leave on the outside light. The light that will stay on throughout the night. I'm not good at secrets and their weight is a constant burden that stops the free-flow of anything else so only by telling myself that the truth will cause even greater pain am I able to hug it tight, and when you're lying close beside me with your arm across my shoulder and insisting again and again that everything will be all right, I can't be the one who breaks this spell with which you seek to protect us all.

The world is tinselled and baubled and time itself is filled with an expectancy to which we can't supply a precise ending. A punter has a ten-thousand-pound bet on with Paddy Power that snow will fall on Christmas Day. And somewhere amidst the arguments about whether last year's John Lewis ad was better than the new one and the city's restaurants and bars filling up with work parties there is a story about a child being born. It's a stupid thing to think but Christmas is a good time for a child to be born and better than the time you chose to come into the world. This unrelenting brightness of snow hurts my eyes. Now the countryside is left behind and I start to pass trading estates, tyre depots and more businesses trying to operate. A man on a quad bike stands upright like a charioteer as he heads along the side of the road.

There is a sense here of the snow being pushed back because commerce needs to continue and because of the heavier flow of traffic. I'm not far away from Luke now and I'm glad because my back is stiff and I'm weary of driving. Even the music has started to sound stale and flat as if I've heard it too many times but I know it's better than what will be playing on the radio.

I waited a week before I started to look for you. Even though your phone is dead Lorna keeps ringing it in the hope that it will suddenly spring into life and hold your voice. Once when she thinks I can't hear she talks quietly into her phone and although I can't make out the words I can guess what she's saying.

'He'll turn up,' I tell her. 'He's probably staying with mates until he gets a flat fixed up. He always turns up.' And you nod because I know you want to believe me.

The city at night is a stranger to me, as I grew up on the Peninsula, and because now we live a short distance outside it I always feel like I'm its foster child rather than one of its natural children. So I'm neither someone who romanticises it nor one who thinks of it only in terms of its bitter histories. But even now as I walk its night streets at a time of our supposed flourishing on the dividends of peace they have an edge to them, some ambiguous quality that you sense in the back of your throat, or on the soles of your shoes, which echo the pavements with both the sound of imagined menace and yet at the same time a friendlier optimism. So you're never sure whether the person coming towards you might wish you harm or want to enfold you in the tightest of embraces. It's a city corralled by mountains and formed at the mouth of the river. Much of it is built on sleech – that mixture of soft grey clay, silt and fine sand up to eight metres deep which in previous centuries meant a forest of timber piles.

They don't use wood any more but bigger buildings now have to be built on a thick bed of piles to anchor their weight on stronger foundations. I read when they constructed the city's newest flagship shopping centre at Victoria Square thousands of piles were used on a site where three hundred years earlier half of it was under the river, while even now below High Street the Farset River curves its secret path to the sea. So perhaps this knowledge fuses with the thoughts in my head to make the random paths I take in the centre's night-time streets feel shifting and, when I walk through the Victoria Centre approaching closing time with its upmarket shops beginning to shut their doors, I think of unseen waters that want to reclaim their stolen domain.

I've started in the university area, showing your photograph to people of similar age and asking if they've seen you, but I worry that it's too dissimilar to how you look now so when they shake their heads I'm not sure if it's because they haven't seen you, or whether it's because they don't recognise you in the image I hold before them. I trawl the student bars around the university and the fast-food outlets along Botanic Avenue, concentrate on the rabbit warren of student-land in what gets called with unintended irony the Holy Land because of its street names – Jerusalem Street, Damascus Street, Carmel Street, Cairo Street, Palestine Street. But everywhere it's a blank. Once in the little square between Upper and Lower Crescent I approach two men drinking on a bench and one looks at the photograph for a long time, but his companion laughs and shakes his head when he says he might have seen you and then asks for money. I give him a couple of pounds; he rubs his chin and tells me he'll keep a lookout for you.

Something happens to me during those nights of searching and it's as if the city begins to exert a compelling power and the world takes on a sharper reality than I have ever known, almost as if everything that's gone before has been clouded and as I look for my son I start to record it. And I find myself increasingly drawn to those unfamiliar city-centre streets whose only purpose seems to be to link to more important places, streets I've never stepped in, and everything in them seems to ask for a moment's recognition. I feel safe in them as if the great spaces of the night and the frantic clamour of the bars and restaurants are contracted into something my hand can touch so I let my fingers brush the brickwork and try to capture their silent emptiness with my camera. Sometimes I think I don't want to go home, go anywhere, but instead make some new kind of life hidden in these secret streets and passageways.

There are times too when I see you – a face glimpsed on the back seat of a late-night bus; a boy, his hood up, with a skateboard under his arm; a young man walking with a skinny dog. At such moments everything courses through me – random unpredictable memories, the words that were spoken, the words that weren't, and then I force myself out of these places of refuge and stare into the crowds, once more show your face to strangers. I tell Lorna that I'm looking for you and as more weeks go by she wants to go to the police or use social media to try and get in touch with you but I persuade her to wait a little longer because you'll be angry and say we've been stupid and that will put even greater distance between us all. I tell her I'll look harder. I promise her I'll look harder.

I check out all the hostels, go to the ones belonging to the Salvation Army where I leave your photograph and my phone number and then enter the waste ground under the bypass where at intervals cars are parked up and from their open windows filter cigarette smoke and the sound of music. Sometimes there is a little pyre of fast-food debris on the ground beside them. Huddles of young people look at me with suspicion and I hide the camera under my coat in case they think I'm a policeman intent on capturing some drug deal. When I show them your photograph they barely look, as if to do so might compromise themselves in the face of their friends, and when I'm walking away I hear a voice saying that if I'm after a boyfriend I should try the Kremlin. Some people I approach think it's a prelude to scamming them for money or collecting for some charity and shrug me off but most are polite and a little embarrassed that they can't help so they walk off quickly and resume their conversations without glancing back. Each night I start in the university area and then end in the city centre.

During these nights I take the photographs – the shadow of railings that have a child's red shoe on one of the spikes, presumably in the hope that it might be reunited with its owner; the white spidery scrawl of new graffiti on a derelict building that has grass and willowherb growing out of its broken crevices; a smeared neon transfer in a shop window that looks like oil in water; the rows of Belfast bikes in their docking station with their grey metal glistening under street lights. And I come to understand the truth of what Ansel Adams said: that you don't make a photograph just with a camera, but that you bring to the act all the pictures you have seen, the books you have read, the music you have heard, the people you have loved. It feels like the closest I've ever been to finding that moment under the surface of things, the closest too that I've ever felt in understanding who you are, as if somehow these photographs also glimpse what exists in you just below your surface. So they're special to me even though I've never shown them to anyone. And I realise that the city itself is a palimpsest, where behind the bland uniformity of chain-store shopfronts is an older and still enduring glimpse of what once was. I see it above the glass where the solidity of red brick and smaller-shaped windows are untouched by time and in my dreams offer the possibility of what might be once more. It makes me wonder if when the snow finally fades the world revealed beneath will remain unchanged or will it be altered in some unexpected way.

These are moments too when the city unfolds itself and offers up its secrets. So what was once only a nondescript shuttered door in daytime reveals itself to be the entrance to a club outside which a line of young people dressed in finery queue for admittance and the small cafe, drab in daylight with its Formica tabletops and plastic chairs, is filled with taxi drivers and revellers stocking up before heading out. For the first time I encounter the city's homeless, those unfortunates sleeping rough in doorways, attempting to insulate themselves against the cold with a base of cardboard and sleeping bags that are grimed and stained. There seem to be about six or seven of these while others who appear to be homeless and beg in spots they have decided might offer the best prospects of charity simply disappear later in the night to what I hope is shelter and a bed. I show your photograph to volunteers running a soup kitchen, but after studying it carefully they apologise for not being able to help. Part of me wants to take photographs of these people sleeping rough, but I can't do it because it feels like I'm a voyeur of someone else's misery and that's never what I want to feel like when I look through a camera, and I can't risk stealing the dignity they still have. Inevitably they make me imagine you transposed to the same situation and then I can't help playing out some of the scenarios based on the conversations I've had with these street sleepers, where the likelihood of kindness from a passer-by is counterbalanced by the possibility of an unprovoked act of violence from those who have consumed too much drink and are laced with the bitterness of disappointment and self-loathing.

From one who tells me his name is Chris I hear the story of a young woman in her thirties who has died during the night. And there have been other deaths too, more than I thought possible. After we talk I go to the shop doorway at the corner of Donegal Place and Castle Lane where she died and take a photograph of an empty space that seems emptier for my presence and I suddenly feel that same space opening up inside me and instead of it spurring me on in my search it drains me of the strength I need so for a couple of nights I can't look any more. It feels like everything's collapsing in on itself at a time when I know I have to be strong, so with the pure assertion of will I force myself to resume. And Lorna's telling me that I need to go back to the doctor, get some of his happy pills, but I can't bring myself to do it because whatever is gained I understand too what gets lost – the blurring of focus that makes things clouded, the dream-riven sleep and above all the loss of the completeness of who you are and what I feel for her. Right now I need to think and see clearly, however difficult that might be.

Luke offers to come with me some nights but I can't let him and know that when I find you we need to be on our own. Lilly does a drawing for you that I'm supposed to deliver. It's got four people in it who may or not be our family and everyone is flying a kite, each one of different colours, and the strings that are attached to them are intertwined which in real life wouldn't be possible but in a ten-year-old's drawing is able to make perfect sense. I think again of those homeless people I encountered and hope that they have all found shelter. And I don't go back at night any more unless it's unavoidable so perhaps now the city has different secrets to reveal and I've never looked again at the photographs I took. I think of it dressed in snow and know that everything I saw will have changed once more. I imagine Luke's drone flying high over the city, seeing the snow topping the green domes of the City Hall, icing the cathedral's new spire, layering the yellow cranes, making the cradle of the mountains white. Does the snow fill those secret streets in which I found a temporary shelter? I pass some kind of warehouse from which young men in blue overalls have spilled out to throw snowballs at each other then find myself behind a car that has reindeer ears attached to its roof. I'm heading south now towards Gateshead on almost the final stage of my journey and I know Luke will be packed and ready to depart.

I turn up on the first few days of term at the art college and ask about you in the main office but they say something about data protection so I have no alternative except to stand and watch students come and go. I tell myself it's easy to pick out the new students, that they have a greater sense of enthusiasm, or is it diffidence? Whichever, it's more likely to be the newer art folders that identify them and the way they haven't yet found a friendship group in which to cluster. On the second day of hanging around I'm approached by a guy who overheard the conversation I had in the office. A lecturer whose name is Alan asks me why I'm looking for you and I say that we haven't heard from you and we're worried. I think he's checking me out, wanting to ascertain whether I represent any kind of threat or have come to cause trouble. Then, when he satisfies himself, he asks your name again and tells me to wait. He's speaking off the record when he informs me that you haven't registered or turned up for the start of your course and after I thank him and begin to walk away he says that he too has a son and wishes me luck. And I think it's luck that finally lets me find you. Through Luke I get access to your Facebook page and find it hasn't been updated for a long time but I start to trawl through old entries and discover three pictures of a girl, one in a Halloween outfit with whitened face, black hair and black lips like someone out of the Addams Family, a selfie taken in some bar with you and the final one with her standing outside a pizza restaurant. She's wearing a black top and black trousers that make me think she might work as a waitress. Only the first three letters of the restaurant's name are visible but they're enough to identify it and I know its location. I've had a birthday meal there with Lorna some years ago so I enlarge the photograph and print it off. She looks about your age and has long auburn hair, piercings in her ears and one in her nose, and above the collar of her black blouse snakes a thin tendril of tattoo. She seems to be mostly called Katty which I assume is a nickname. I don't have a second name and although I search through Facebook I can't find her. So I take the photograph to the restaurant just before it opens and they tell me that she used to work there but don't any more and anyway they couldn't give out personal information. But when they're talking amongst themselves I overhear a second name and when I go back to Facebook I'm able to find her account but can't access it because it's set to private. I ask to befriend her and before she accepts she sends me a DM asking who I am. I tell her and say I'd be really grateful if she was prepared to speak to me.

Her hair is a different colour from the photograph but I have no trouble recognising her when we meet in the cafe of her choice. Her name is Kate.

'You know Daniel, don't you?'

'I did but I haven't seen him for some time now,' she says without looking at me directly and sipping the coffee I've bought her. 'Is he in trouble?'

'No, he's not in trouble – it's just we haven't seen him for a good while and we want to find out if he's all right. He was supposed to start his course at the art college and he hasn't turned up. We're worried about him.'

She nods but doesn't reply at first, as if she's weighing up the pros and cons of helping me. So I try not to pressurise her and instead ask her how she knew you.

'We met at a friend's party. We got on pretty well – we were both doing art in school so it gave us something to talk about. But we never became really close or anything. Danny was a good laugh – that's all. Never took anything too serious.'

Now it's my turn to nod to show I recognise the person she's talking about and to hide my impatience. She seems nervous and despite what I've done to try and put her at ease that nervousness seems to be increasing. I'm about to cut to the chase and ask her if she knows where I can find you when she holds her cup with both hands and without raising her eyes from it reveals the things that have made her uneasy.

'I really liked Danny; for a little while when I first met him I thought we could have amounted to more than friends but ... there were other things I didn't like. And maybe you know this already but he didn't have good friends, didn't hang round with people who were going to be good for him.'

'People who did drugs?'

'A lot of people do drugs but they do the right ones. Know what I'm saying. Danny, and I don't really know why, started to do the wrong drugs. Drugs that rub you up against bad people and drugs that aren't about fun but something else. And he took risks.'

She looks up at me briefly then glances round the cafe. A strand of hair that has fallen across her face is pushed behind an ear. When she moves her head her metal piercings catch the light.

'We really need to find him. To help him,' I tell her. 'Do you know where he is?'

She shakes her head slowly and I can't decide whether she's telling me the truth or not.

'Please help us, Kate.'

'I haven't had any contact with him in a long time, haven't even seen him since before the summer. I'd like to help you but don't think I can.'

'Where was he staying when you were friends?'

'Somewhere up round the university, somewhere in the Holy Land but I never went there and don't know where exactly. I'm sorry.'

And then she's gone with a haste that suggests she's worried that she's said too much and I've hardly time to thank her before she's disappeared into the street.

So I go back to the same starting place every night and sift the faces of the throngs of students whose numbers are now added to by other new arrivals from a mixture of ethnic backgrounds. I become familiar to the wardens who patrol the area seeking to stop the antisocial behaviour of mostly students that has plagued the original residents for decades. I pass houses where the accommodation looks worse than basic and which have been subdivided again and again to maximise rent returns. If anyone recognises you they won't admit it and probably think they are showing the solidarity of youth and why should they identify what might be one of their own to someone who's old enough to be their own father?

It rains one night and there are fewer people about. I take shelter under one of the trees that line the street and think of going home but can't face the expectancy on your mother's face when I come through the door and then the disappointment that will replace it. I'm passed by three young men seemingly impervious to the rain, one of them carrying a pack of beer cans, the second wheeling what looks like a kid's BMX bike and the third three boxes of pizza. They're wearing a kind of uniform of Canterbury tracksuit bottoms and hoodies and even when they're talking to each other they're looking at their phones. Then they stop and stare up at the houses and they're arguing about something I can't make out. When they see me under the tree one of them speaks to me.

'All right, mate? We're looking for Declan's place. Declan Rourke. His place is somewhere round here but we don't know the number. Do you know him?'

'Sorry. Can you not phone him?'

'The bastard isn't answering his phone. Anyone would think he doesn't want us at his party.'

The one with the bike asks me if I want to buy it and I say sorry again and then they're gone, their phone screens little glimmers in the dusk. As they walk they look up at all the windows with lights on and stand listening for the sounds of revelry. I think of going after them and showing your photograph but decide not to and am increasingly resigned to returning home with another failure written on my face. A woman wearing a hijab and carrying two bags of shopping goes wearily by.

The rain is heavier now and two young women pass me, leaning shoulder to shoulder under an umbrella that has broken spokes, and they give little squeals when they get splashed. I watch them cross the road and enter the convenience store on the opposite street corner. Then in my final attempt of the night I follow them, narrowly avoiding the spray from a passing bus and beginning to feel an increasing coldness seeping into my core.

The shop is crowded but no one is buying more than a couple of items that they carry away in their hands and because it's so busy it makes it difficult to show any of the staff your photograph until I notice an older man I guess is the manager standing to the side of the tills with a cup of coffee in his hand. When I show him, it's obvious he recognises you and he looks at it and then at me as to find the resemblance, then sets his coffee down on the counter.

'Danny Boy. Yeah, I know Danny. You say you're his father?'

When I tell him yes he shakes his head slowly and at first I think it's an expression of sympathy but then he says, 'Good luck to you with that. He doesn't come in here any more because he's barred. He was lucky I didn't call the police because it sure as hell wasn't the first time he robbed me.'

'I'm sorry,' I tell him and offer to pay for whatever was stolen but he shrugs the offer away. 'Have you any idea where I might find him? It's really important.'

'I know where I'd like to find him.'

It's obvious he wants his pound of flesh and so I apologise again and try to give him twenty pounds but he shakes his head.

'He's not the only one round here. They have their money spent halfway through the first term and if Bank of Mum and Dad doesn't bail them out they're in here thinking it's a charity shop. Put your money away – it's not you owes me but if you see him tell him he's still barred.'

I promise I will and when I ask again if he knows where I might find you he turns to call to one of his staff on the till and the answer comes back, 'Somewhere in Palestine Street.'

'Somewhere in Palestine Street,' he says in case I haven't heard and then lifts his cup again.

It's only a five-minute walk away through the rain that continues to fall and which shines the road and the roofs of the houses. There are fewer people about – a couple of women jogging, someone riding a bike with no lights. A few of the houses have skips outside them and are being renovated or cleared out. The narrow street runs down towards the river and it feels as if a dampness has ebbed from it to lap round the red-bricked houses and the cars parked outside them. The dampness and the rain make the houses seem blurred into each other and everything feels unfocused. I don't know where to start but for some reason walk to the lower part of the street where there are more For Rent signs.

Two men, maybe Romanians, are having an argument over a car, with one of them looking as if he is indicating its defects, and at one point he slaps its roof, jewelling a little spray of water that splashes into the air. When I approach I have to wait until they finish shouting at each other and become aware of my presence. I apologise for disturbing them and show the photograph. They confer with each other and I think they're going to argue again but then the younger man gestures to a house across the street and when I point at the one I think he's indicated he nods vigorously before launching into their argument once more.

The curtains in the front room are pulled tight. From the fanlight above the solid door leaks a soiled yellow light. I ring the bell but hear nothing inside so I knock and then knock again. Eventually the door is opened only wide enough for a man to see me without revealing much of himself. I try to explain but he shakes his head as if he thinks I'm looking to sell him something and he's going to close the door until I hold the photograph up to the sliver of light. The door is opened to me. The hall I'm standing in has two bicycles leaning against the wall, some stacked cartons of what looks like cooking oil, and laced through everything is a pungent smell of cooking and something that might be drains. He doesn't speak but simply points up the flight of stairs.

There is a cheap spongy carpet on the stairs and on some steps it sags loosely outwards so I climb carefully and slowly. The walls are covered with flocked floral wall-paper that looks as if it's been there from the seventies and in places it has tears where something's snagged it. Halfway up I stop and think of going back. The man who opened the door has disappeared into the front room from where I hear the sound of a television. So stop now, retrace your steps and walk back outside to where the wet streets now hold out the chance of a return to the world as it was once before.

This is the last moment when the story can be told a different way, when the images that you carry printed on your memory can be arranged in a different pattern, and if the outcome can't be changed then there's still time to come to it by a different and maybe better path. Something that might offer the hope of more understanding or a greater prospect of comfort. Steps on the stairs. Sometimes they become the steps of Luke's house on which I climb up two floors to where his room nestles under the roof and which he was pleased about because he thought it was big and gave him more privacy. Now he waits there for me to arrive. Waits for me to take him home. At other times they are the stairs of our home which I climb only after checking all the doors and making sure the front one is unchained and the outside porch light remains turned on, because when I get in beside Lorna she will ask if I've remembered. And if there is a night when I've forgotten she will throw back the duvet and go down the same stairs, each resolute press of her bare foot a rebuke for my carelessness. Denis Thorpe's photograph in Lowry's hallway taken after the painter's death when he came across men starting to clear the house and persuaded them to let him record the interior. Two coats and hats in a shadowed hallway. Flock wallpaper. I touch it with my hand and then pull away at its coldness.

Afterwards when everything has been done a policewoman drives me back to where I've parked my car. She asks if she can phone someone who might come and drive me home but I tell her that I can do it. She touches my arm before she leaves. I feel it deeply, aware even briefly in that second that I still exist as a physical being, because from that moment the material world gives up its reality as life now ebbs and flows only as an inescapable welter of thought and image. But when she's gone I can't get in the car, can't take this thing home to my family. I'm not ready. I walk down to the river in a desperate attempt to steady myself long enough to make the journey home to prepare myself for what I must say. Its surface is pimpled by the rain and I hold tightly to the railings, try to find once again the reality, however brief, that I still exist in a body. The water looks dark but is oiled and smeared in places with a jittery skim of light. Your skin bruised and discoloured as if whatever corruption and decay unravel inside you are seeping steadily to the surface and the light edging in from the street is unable to quicken you into life or second chance. I know that from the moment I open the door. It's in the frozen fix of your body's shape on the mattress, a locked and rigid stillness that makes me cry out, cry your name because I can't recognise that stillness in you, have no memory of you ever held in such a grasp. And the room is bare, with little more than a single chair that holds your clothes, a second mattress and a wardrobe with its missing door revealing that it contains nothing but a few metal hangers. I say your name again and again and louder each time as if you are a small child once more and I am calling you back to safety. Back from the high places, the sea that is too rough. Back to love. Come even now, Daniel, walking towards me across this snow-filled road, and I'll stop the car for you, blast the heater to warm you. Take you home.

'Are you all right, mate?' a man asks. He's stopped jogging because he's thinking I might be about to go into the water.

'I'm fine, thanks,' I tell him, trying to stem the waver of my voice. 'Just looking at the river.'

'I can stay with you, look at the river with you,' he says and his high-vis vest hurts my eyes.

'That's good of you,' I tell him, 'but I'm heading home now. Have a good run.'

He stands by the railings until I start to walk away. And have I ever thought of going in the water since that night? Yes I've thought about it, and had times in the hours before dawn when sleep has deserted me or when out driving on my own it's whispered to me, but it's not a voice I'll ever listen to because I have a family who need me, need me more than ever, and so I have to find strength from wherever it can be found to keep on. Just as I'm keeping on this road to bring Luke home. A mattress and a sleeping bag. That's all. No paraphernalia we see in films – no needles or tourniquets, no lighter or silver foil, no pipes or small spoons. The bareness of that room. Each time I go into yours that Lorna is not ready yet to change I remember it and it tries to shape itself into this space we thought of as belonging to you, pushing aside the older memories the room wants to hold. They aren't able to say what made your heart give out. There are traces of many different things. And none of it matters. Lilly wants to see you but it's a closed lid because you've gone beyond what might be done to make that possible. All of us are smaller, drawn inwards to silence because we don't know what it is we should say to each other, and all of us are frightened because as we stand at the graveside we encounter full face the shuddering dominion of death. A father and now a son in this place so I stand in a no man's land between what should have been the future and the past that was and I don't know to which I belong. It troubles me that Luke is going to return there and make his film but I know I'll go with him and help him in whatever way he needs, if he needs my help at all.

Sometime in the weeks afterwards Lilly puts an app on my phone. Everyone in her class has it and what it does is measure how many footsteps you take in a day. She tells me I'm supposed to do ten thousand. But it comes to record only my inertia, the pathetic number of steps I take, because now everything feels as if it has shut down and can't be stirred into motion. Sleeping, staring at the television with its sound turned down low and without any awareness of what I'm watching. Even getting out of the chair to go to my studio takes on the appearance of an arduous trek fraught with obstacles and dangers. And the world is too loud – the sound of the vacuum cleaner, the washing machine's final manic screaming spin, even the clean cutlery being dropped into the kitchen drawer. All of it lacerates, all of it makes me feel as if I want to swim in perfect silence under the surface of deep water, for the ice to close over my head. For Lorna it's different. The very opposite. She can't sit still and she's set herself in a motion that she must hope will stem what's inside and at any moment is at risk of overflowing and drowning her. So she's set her feet on surer ground and she's washing and cleaning, stripping the beds and beating the house into a shape because she says it's been neglected and everywhere is beginning to look run-down and in need of attention. I want to beg her to stop but I can't and so I try to separate myself from the noise she's making as if she thinks it might scatter the spirits that have settled on our home. And sometimes Lilly makes us both reveal the number of steps we've taken and the gap is so great that there are times when I wonder if we can ever survive this thing or if every day we're stepping further away from each other.

We choose photographs for the funeral service that are projected on to the wall behind the speaker to the sound of Moby's 'Porcelain'. People don't understand photographs. They think they always freeze the moment in time but the truth is that they set the moment free from it and what the camera has caught steps forever outside its onward roll. So it will always exist, always live just as it was in that precise second, with the same smile or scowl, the same colour of sky, the same fall of light and shade, the very same thought or pulse of the heart. It's the most perfect thing that sets free the eternal in the sudden stillness of the camera's click. I find a comfort in that and I'll take comfort anywhere it offers itself. Those that Lorna chooses are of Daniel in a different time and they all show a boy still holding tightly to happiness. I understand that and I like them too. But the final two projected on the wall are the most recent and in neither of them do we see his face. The first is on the bridge when he was walking across, because I took it before he saw me and he's walking away across a chasm of space towards the other side, and the second is of him standing on the stones looking out at the sea, dwarfed by its immensity and power. These are the ones that tear at my heart because he's on his own, just as he was at the end when I should have been there in that room, taking back the words I spoke in fear and anger, taking my son back to his family.

The traffic slows and eventually comes to a stop. At first I can't see the cause of the delay then as we begin to edge forward I see a policeman with a light-stick calming and directing the flow. As I get closer I see his light-stick has a little garland of tinsel round the handle. I lower my window and he tells me a lorry has jackknifed and just to keep my speed down and follow directions. But we soon come to a complete standstill as they let traffic flow from the opposite direction. I check there's no police about and phone Lorna because I want nothing more than to hear her voice.

'Everything all right?' she asks and I realise that ringing her instinctively makes her think something bad has happened.

'Everything's fine. I'm not far away now. But I'm sitting in traffic because some lorry up ahead has blocked the road.'

'Will you still be in time to get the boat?'

'I think so and if we're not we'll still be able to get the later sailing.'

'They say the airport is opening again.'

'Murphy's Law but most of the flights between now and Christmas are booked up – there's no guarantee that we could have got him on one.'

'Luke phoned, says he's started to feel a bit better. But make sure he keeps drinking and takes those tablets.'

'He just needs to get home, get a bit of TLC. He'll be fine.'

The traffic still hasn't moved. Some of the cars coming towards me have their sidelights on and I take their example. There is a moment of silence before I ask, 'Have you turned the outside lights on yet?'

'They're on. I'll keep them on so Luke can see them if you get home late.'

'How are you?' I ask suddenly, almost before I know I'm going to do it.

'So-so. Up and down. I'll be better when you're both home.'

'How's Lilly?'

'Pretty excited. We've been doing some baking. The kitchen's a mess.'

'Can you put her on?'

I hear Lorna tell her that her father wants to speak to her.

'Hi, Lilly.'

'Where are you now?'

'Not far away. Almost there.'

'It's taken you a long time. Luke will be tired waiting.'

'It's a long journey. What are you baking?'

'Shortbread shaped like holly leaves.'

'Very good. Maybe we'll see you on *The Great British Bake Off* with Mary Berry or you'll be the new Mary Holly Berry.'

'Very funny.'

Silence and then the next voice I hear is Lorna's.

'OK, Tom. Drive safe and don't rush to catch the next sailing if it's better to take your time and get home safely. Even if it's the last one I'll be waiting up. I've lots of things to do. Things to wrap that I can't do while you-know-who's about.'

I say goodbye without asking her what was in my head — if we are going to make it, keep our heads above the water, how we can keep our children safe every day for the rest of our lives. If she will be able to forgive me. I wanted too to say that I am going to try harder this Christmas than I have ever tried before no matter what

I feel inside. I promise it aloud in the silence of the car and grip the steering wheel more tightly as if to make the words a physical reality.

We start to move again but slowly and then enter a chicane of orange cones, passing the jackknifed lorry as a policewoman beckons us on and inevitably every driver's head turns to stare. It doesn't look to have crashed into anything more solid than a stretch of scrubland and nothing has spilled from it. I think of Rosemary and wonder how's she doing and whether any of her injuries have proved more serious than she thought and I wonder too if she will be cared for by her daughter who nurses in the hospital. Strange to be nursed by your child but I guess that reversal of roles is one that probably awaits us all down the road. And I wonder why Luke wants to film in the cemetery and whether he's been infected by some morbid fascination with the rituals of death. Although I didn't say to him, I know the section he's talking about because I walked through it one afternoon when my mother had asked me to check that my father's headstone had been done as requested. The cemetery is taken up mostly by traditional graves where no decorations are allowed so that the grass can be cut, but on the other side of the road exists this strange area of trees where families have personalised the final resting place of their loved ones so it's a sea of glass-covered photographs, soft toys and mementoes, suncatchers, wind mobiles, hanging crystals, ribbons and streamers tied to branches. Scarves and items associated with favoured football teams feature a lot and there are memorials to babies who have died. It's a strange place and the talismanic offerings give it the feel of something more primitive and superstitious and, despite the modern objects, of you having ventured into some ancient burial site that rests outside the conventional world.

The road ahead is clear now, and the satnav tells me I'll be at Luke's in twenty-five minutes, but even though I've started to consider what we might talk about, the music we might listen to, that's not where I'm going any more. I haven't planned this. It doesn't make any sense. But something stronger than sense is making me turn off the road, reconfigure the satnav even though I almost hear its bewilderment at this last-minute change to the journey it's mapped out so precisely for me. I saw it a few minutes ago, suddenly rearing up, insistently bigger than any picture can conceive, and I tell myself that it won't take long. That there's still time. There'll still be time for me to find my son and take him home. I'm not a religious person but I think of those who have travelled across deserts and dusty plains, following what comes down to faith and then finding the journey ends in a place none of them has ever expected. I have no faith but there have been times when I wondered if one could find me because it offers things that aren't open to anyone without it. Things that look good to this person I've become. So there's the possibility of forgiveness, of your sins being white as the purest of this snow, of thinking everything is part of a plan that although bewildering in the present will make sense in the future. Of having the pain taken away. Being given something to follow other than your own craziness and something to guide you to what I remember the minister at my father's graveside called 'blessed assurance'.

I don't possess that blessed assurance, don't think I ever will, but wherever it's coming from I know I have to follow where this impulse is taking me. And perhaps that's the only form of faith open to me now so I can't ignore it or write it off as the confusion that has come to dominate every part of my life. And for the first time since this thing happened I want to take a photograph because maybe, if I can do that right, other things might come right too. Take a photograph of this Angel that rises high above everything and whose wings exercise a dominion over all below. So I follow the directions given to me by a woman whose voice has brought me safely this far but who I've never seen – is it possible that she alone in the world now understands what veers me off my pre-planned route and brings me the short distance to the car park where there is only one other car? The light is beginning to drop and I can tell from the footsteps in the snow that many people have been there during the day and I see tracks that look like some kids have had a sledge.

A text comes through on my phone. It's from Rosemary and says, 'Tom, nothing broken. Being kept in overnight as precaution but getting home in the morning. Hope you and Luke get home safely. Once again a big thanks. Have a good Christmas, Rosemary.' I tell her I'm pleased for her and wish her well but not where I am. I can't tell anyone where I am because it's not where I'm supposed to be and I can't explain the reason if anyone asks.

When I get out of the car I feel a stiffness in my legs and back as I put on my coat and zip the collar up high against the coldness that suddenly floods around me. I search for my gloves but can't find where I've left them. A young couple are coming down from the monument with two young children scampering ahead of them and kicking flurries of snow with their wellingtons. A smoke of breath is on all their lips and as we pass we wish each other a Merry Christmas like we're characters in a Dickens story.

My own two boys – the pride once felt in those words echoing back down the years – and they're young and brimming full of excitement at camping in Tollymore Forest, so much that they scamper and skip as if their bodies can't be contained in the confines of a normal walk and we know we have to tire them out if any of us are to have a chance of getting a sleep during the coming night. So we bring them along the river and through the forest and they're throwing stones into the white rush of water and clambering down to look for fish in the shadows below the grey slabs of rock on the other bank. Words of caution on their parents' lips, but smiles too, and their excitement is infectious so we also feel free and part of me wants to show off to them, to let them see that I too can share in something of what races through them. The very best phase, when that shared excitement is still possible and new experience is there to be embraced and nothing needs to be forced and it's as if you're looking at the world for the first time. Seeing it as a child.

As the family starts to unload their stuff into the boot of the car the two boys kick snow at each other while their parents coax them to stand still long enough for them to unzip their coats. My own children have spotted a tiny fish and urge us to follow them down to the gravelly edge of the water, but we can't see it at first, even though they're pointing and shouting, because our eyes aren't sharp and wide like theirs and because the shadows mottle the surface. Suddenly their voices have the exasperation of the parent whose child can't see what they can and then we do and they're so pleased as if they've revealed something of the world's magic to us. As if they've taught us how to see. Then we put our hands under their arms and pretend to swing them out over the water to catch the fish so that they're squealing with pretend fear and our bodies are linked like they'll never be again. Swinging out over the water. Held safe.

I watch the car drive away, its throaty exhaust a momentary dark spume against the white. The air is cold against my face and pinches my ears but for a few seconds of memory I feel the sun slanting through the trees and skimming a swathe of light across the surface of the water where in its reflections trembles a welter of tiny insects. A dragonfly. Another small fish. A piece of branch like a little boat carried downstream. We'll pitch our tent here and live inside the moment so there's no need to be swept along by time. I know you like it here and yes we can learn how to fish and build fires. So let's stay safe in this moment and let nothing ever take us away from it.

Here are stepping stones that ford the river set at regular intervals and between which the water courses and tumbles to the white-frothed level below. A challenge that has to be taken up but the stones are regular and broad, solid underfoot, so it's not difficult enough and then you're offering each other challenges and it begins with hopping on one leg and despite your parents' warnings you're determined to show your bravery and, even when Lorna tells you to stop, Daniel says he's going to cross it with his eyes closed and although I'm telling him not to be stupid and that he'll fall he simply strides across with perfectly measured steps and we don't know whether to be cross or applaud. When Luke who feels outshone goes to emulate his brother's feat we both grab hold of him and forbid it. Lorna presses him tightly into her and we all stare at the seemingly unstoppable flow of the water.

Night walks through the city. Young people sparked by a sense of excitement in the Cathedral Quarter with the girls' heels struggling on the cobbled streets. The city flows here like the river below it. Who can tell where it will take us? Searching every face but looking for what? A chance encounter? For my son? For something else for which I do not have a name? Bars and restaurants extend an invitation with the light arcing from their windows and doorways but it feels as if something prevents me from ever entering. Groups spill outside to drink under the strings of outdoor lights, the young people dressed as if the night isn't cold. As I get closer to the Angel my hands are shaking and I don't know why. Is every son destined to become his father? Are these shaking hands his afterlife in me? Sometimes in a mirror, when I catch myself by chance, I think it's his face giving back my reflection and it's into him that time bears me ever closer. At the end I wanted to hoop him with my arms, not out of love, but to hold him so tightly that his tremble I felt passing into me would be stilled and the world fall back into balance. And I do not want my son ever to be me and, despite whatever's happening inside, never let him see my body tremble and if he can do it let him hold me only in love. Let him be better than his father, with a surer grasp of happiness.

The paths to the monument have disappeared under the snow but I follow where others have walked and as

I head up to it through the trees whose branches look as if they have fossilised into a white coral its wings seem to suddenly reach out over my head although I am still at a distance. Despite the vastness of its scale the body that is angled towards my approach is wholly human in its muscled leg, the swell of its buttock, the tilt of its head but it's the ribbed wings that press their immensity on the landscape, the sky, what you feel inside. This is something I have to do but right now my hands are shaking too badly to take the photograph. I don't have much time and the light is ebbing. I want to hear the sound of my family's voices but I can't ring them without them knowing that I've stopped on my journey. Another promise that they'll think I've broken.

Sometimes I can't help thinking that the night we smoked the bats out of their hidden place and sent them skittering and frantic into the dark was the moment that I disturbed some natural order, set in motion everything that has ever happened in my life. But I tell myself that it's a weakness to look for something to blame, a weakness in me that no pill is ever going to cure. And if I am to tell myself the truth I no longer believe that any order exists and if it ever did it's broken and no matter how hard we try we'll never be able to put it together again. A quickening of shame too as I remember the times I've let myself think of going under but as I look up at the Angel I know it's not my body I now want to put into the pure white grave of snow but the bad things I've done, the mistakes I've made, the flaws that seeded themselves in me and which I let grow. Each word that was spoken. That's what I want to bury in this place that feels as sacred as anywhere I've ever stood.

The temperature is dropping. Young men and women sleeping in the city's crevices. Let shelter be found for them. Let those who come stop on their journey at a shop doorway where a young woman died. See too a bare room with two mattresses.

Sleeping bags for bedclothes. An empty wardrobe. I look at my hands with their blunt fingers that hold this camera and remember Stieglitz's portraits of O'Keeffe's hands – in all of them the hands are alive, expressive, beautiful. Your hands when I first held you and wondered how life could be replicated and reduced to such perfection, thinking that they had been freshly sculpted from wet clay. My own son's hands, the physical embodiment of the life I helped bring into the world. Nothing has ever matched the strength of that awareness. Not in the album of photographs. Not in the giving back to the earth.

I try desperately to arrange happy memories from childhood around your head but they can't fasten to you and fall away. I'm clutching for something to hold on to. To stop myself from falling. I think of you on the rope bridge walking across that chasm of space and air and how you had no fear, how you never had any fear, and I hope above all that in those final moments you closed your eyes and were spared its touch as you set out across. A vapour trail sears itself into the sky. The planes are flying again and although the snow will slip away in time I want it to stay long enough so that we shut ourselves in over this holiday and hold each other safe. I think of the fire that Lorna has lit and the lights outside our house and draw enough strength from these images to steady my hands and take the photograph of the Angel. I want its scale, its strength, the span of its wings, want to carry the image wherever I go in the future. And I've decided I'm going to show the photographs I shot on those nights and perhaps they'll be my final offering to you if you'll only accept them and know that each of those steps was taken with love.

There's something I need to do now that I've not been able to do even though I've tried so many times before. I've carried it with me every day, every single day and known it's there, thought about it so much that it's become a part of this person I've become. But I've never looked, not once, because if I did it might be what brings everything tumbling down and even now in the solitude of this place I search for some way out of what must be done, ask that this thing might be taken from me. The colour is draining from the sky but there are still broken patches of blue and I stand looking at them and listening to the sound of the traffic, hoping to hear a voice that might guide me. The Angel that came to visit Joseph told him not to be afraid because what was conceived was of the Holy Spirit and I tell myself I must quell my fear and do this thing. That it was conceived in a father's love. So I take my camera and find the file that's well hidden and open the picture I took of my dead son. My last photograph of my son. I force myself to look at it, try to think of some prayer to say, but no words come and then I press delete and let him go.

I drop to my knees and try to stop myself being sick by scooping a handful of snow and pressing it against my mouth. If anyone were to come now and see me it would look as if I was bowing to the Angel, supplicating myself to the magnitude that stands before me. My father's tremble has burrowed inside me, shivering every part of my being.

I retch but nothing comes and only through the exercise of sheer willpower do I manage to stop myself from yielding to the snow's whispered invitation to sleep.

Then I hear Lorna's voice all those years ago telling me to look at my son with my eye and as I lift my face that's what I try to do. With my eye. Only with my eye. A boy crossing stepping stones, his own eyes closed. A boy almost knocking me over in his haste to enter the living room on Christmas morning. His badly wrapped presents for his mother and father – a pair of woollen gloves for me, perfume for Lorna. The music that once came from his room. Telling me with a smile on his face that he'd just met a girl who said that when Bob Marley sang that everything was going to be all right she believed him. Really believed him. The boy catching a wave on his bodyboard, his smiling face raised to us as he races towards the shore on its breaking crest. That day we were in the car and we sat looking at the sea with the chips in their wrapping, our fingers salted and warm. Crossing the bridge when I alone felt the fear. Three paintings he did of the old man – the old man that one day I shall be, with a life that exists only in memories. The secret hidden places in the city where I once sought shelter and through which now he might walk once more with his father if he allows me to show them to the world.

I look up at the Angel that offers shelter under its wings but I know there is another photograph I want to take so I try to breathe myself into a greater calm then slowly get up from the snow. I walk back the way I've come, return to the car and because it seems to bristle with impatience tell it that it will only have to wait a few more minutes. A few more minutes before I make the final leg of my journey and find my son. Then I lift Lilly's wigwam from the boot and walk back up between the trees and, when I'm halfway there, there is a sudden silent blur of movement through the air and it's a white-faced owl coming straight over my head and in a blink it's gone but its afterimage forms almost immediately, forming as if from some negative to be stored in the darkroom of memory. Printed with filaments from this fading sun.

And I could tell myself as I set a child's wigwam on the crest of the hill under the wings that I've done it to show scale or to bring some token of my family to this holy place for a blessing but as I open and safely anchor it, look at its painted ponies, the moons and stars, I can't explain it in words. So as I walk down the slope and take the photograph it reveals itself only as a mystery but now I think its mystery is all that's left.

Everything is done now so let me shelter under these wings as I touch the Angel's feet, sense its foundations, the concrete piles that anchor it to the earth, the wings that don't flutter no matter how strong the wind and which somehow point to the future. Then I do something I've never done since childhood and say a prayer, a secret prayer, because I've finally found the words. When it's finished and with the sun dropping ever lower I know that I have to go, that I have to journey on and bring my son home – the son to whom I'm bringing no wisdom but instead some chocolate from an old woman he'll never meet, the music that he likes and all the remedies and charms his mother has garnered to make him well. I'm coming now, Luke, and if God does really keep score, let him record that I'm going to continue my journey until I finally get to hear the voice that has brought me safely here, say, *You have reached your destination*. The world is growing colder. I start to lift the wigwam but then something tells me I have to leave it, that this is where it belongs, and I hope that Lilly will somehow come to understand, understand that her father left it here for the homeless, for every soul in need of shelter and, as the sun finally sets over this snow-covered world, for every fellow traveller, lost like him in a strange land.

A NOTE FROM THE AUTHOR

You can listen to some of the music referenced on Tom's journey here: http://spoti.fi/2AmKBko

In a creative collaboration with the author, the award-winning photographer Sonya Whitefield has created a personal response to *Travelling in a Strange Land* that combines image and text. You can view these photographs at www.sonyawhitefield.com